DIRTY FLIRT

A SLAYERS HOCKEY NOVEL

MIRA LYN KELLY

Photographer: J. Ashley Converse

Model: Dane Peterson

Cover Designer: Najla Qamber, Najla Qamber Designs

Editor: Jennifer Miller

For my Family

1

Off-Season

"**L**ittle Dude, I thought it'd end different for you." I heave a breath, shaking my head as I carry the fallen soldier to my bathroom. "Saw you going out in a blaze of glory. Belly full of the good stuff. Final hours spent in the land of milk and honey."

Jesus, I haven't had to toss an expired rubber since high school.

Back then, my girlfriend kept saying she wanted to *do it* then changing her mind. Fair. No one should do anything before they're ready, so I never pressured her. Ever. I was good with waiting, good with throwing away one unopened box of condoms a year for three years straight... until I found out said girlfriend had been *doing* Steven Huang since New Year's our senior year.

Yeouch.

Next time I bought a box of rubbers, I was back to buy a second box less than twelve hours later.

Been that kind of steady turnover ever since. At least until six months ago when my left nut went rogue and—

"Yo, Boomer, got a minute?"

I turn to where my teammate, roommate, and bromantic bestie, Grant Bowie, is leaning against the doorjamb. "Dude, moment of silence here?"

He closes his eyes, but instead of acknowledging the loss like a normal human being, the guy who stole my little sister runs a hand over his face and groans. "Knock off the somber bullshit. Condoms don't expire in one year."

Rude.

"Not by the manufacturer's standards, but I like to keep a solid buffer between me and the edge of *iffy*... especially when it comes to protection."

He considers and gives me a nod. "Okay. For you, that's probably good practice. But your sister wants to talk. Let's go."

Ignoring the dig, I toss the rubber and follow Bowie out to the front of the apartment where Piper's sitting at the table she made us buy because she was sick of eating on the couch or floor and felt that as professional hockey players in the NHL, we could definitely afford it. She's got a glass of water in front of her and a sweet smile on her face that reminds me of when she was little. Cute. Not dating my teammate.

Good times.

Bowie drops a kiss at her temple and slides onto the chair beside her while I take the one across from them. "This about your trip? Need a ride to the airport?"

They've already shared their itinerary, and Bowie promised to hit a couple virtual workouts with me while they're gone.

"No, we're all set. There's something else, Ben."

Uh-oh. "My hockey gear?"

She glances at the clothesline I strung across the living room last week to air out my equipment... and possibly just to see what she'd say because I'm maybe still the tiniest bit butthurt about the fact that she's usurped me as the most important person in Bowie's life.

"No. It's not about the gear." She levels me with a look. "But that's gross and you should put it away."

I'm planning on it. Eventually. "The oatmeal? Because I learned my lesson about leaving it in the bowl, and the new dishes are going to be here tomorrow."

"What?" she chokes as Bowie's head whips toward the kitchen.

Not the oatmeal then. "They're really nice."

My sister nods. Sighs and then smiles.

And that's when I notice the boxes.

Oh shit. "Just what exactly is happening here?"

"Ben, listen," she says with a voice so calm I think I might puke, because no good thing comes from that soothing tone. "We're getting our own place."

TWENTY-FOUR HOURS LATER, I'm back at the table where they broke the news to me, freaking the fuck out. I've been abandoned. Piper and Bowie are gone.

I tried everything to sway them not to go...

Tantrums.

Ultimatums.

Sulking.

But apparently, they'd been prepared for all that and worse, which is why they didn't tell me about their move until they were ready to leave. I mean, I wouldn't *actually* have sabotaged their plans. But I've met me, and I guess I can see why they might think maybe I would.

Whatever.

They left yesterday. I don't like it, but surprisingly enough, that's not the part that has me losing my shit. No. It's that in some misguided attempt to soften the blow of bailing on me, my little sister took it upon herself to find me a replacement roommate.

Umm... WTF, Piper. W... T... F.

But when I protested, she just smacked a kiss on my cheek acting like she'd given me the biggest present under the tree instead of my eight-years-estranged, side-bestie from high school.

Lara Elliot.

I pull up my photos and drag my thumb through the years until I'm back in high school. Piper's still a lanky kid who hasn't grown into her looks yet. Bowie's a year ahead of me and already drafted. My Juniors team is filled with guys dreaming of a career only a couple will achieve. And Lara's filling up half the pictures. Brown eyes dancing, blonde hair blowing in the wind. A hundred different smiles, because nothing got that girl down.

We walked through fire together, and I'd counted her as one of my best friends before life took us in two different directions.

That's all it was... I think.

College for her. Hockey for me.

Life.

No fight. No bad blood.

Nothing but time and distance and a series of small decisions each with their own course-changing conse-quences doing what they do... even though we'd sworn they wouldn't.

"Tell me this won't change things."

A breathless whisper in the night.

"Friends forever, Elle. Nothing's changing that."

Now it's been eight years. No phone call. No text. Not a single slide into my DMs.

Just a conversation with my little sister, and suddenly this woman I don't even know anymore is moving into my apartment... sometime in the next hour-ish.

It's a bullshit move, the kind of thing the girl I knew in high school never would have pulled. But even as epically uncool as it is that she hasn't bothered to check in with me directly... I'm still going to let her move in. Because time and distance and all they've done aside, I don't like the idea of her showing up in a new city and not having someone she knows to stay with.

We're not talking about forever here. Couple days, maybe a week until she finds a new place.

But yeah. I should probably take the clothesline down.

Lara

STANDING in front of the door to what's supposed to be my new apartment, spinner bag at my side, key in one hand and phone in the other, I quietly hyperventilate.

"Mother*fucker*."

Okay, not so quietly. Or politely. Or professionally, which is a problem considering the only reason I'm in

Chicago at all is to keep on killing it at the PR firm Giles, Hall, & Wren. To prove that I've got the stuff to move up to the New York office. Something I've been so focused on that in the chaos of these last few days, I somehow screwed up this one not-so-insignificant thing.

I read the text from Piper Boerboom again, her shouty caps turning my insides to knots.

PIPER: OMG!! YOU THOUGHT YOU WERE MOVING IN WITH ME???!!! I AM SO SORRY!

THERE ARE A DOZEN MORE TEXTS, sent in rapid fire. Explanations about an out-of-country vacation, an apartment that opened up in the building, and how she and Grant Bowie— I did not see *that* relationship coming! —had to move on it quickly. She'd been distracted and rushing, and when she offered me the room in the apartment her brother owned, she wasn't clear about the fact that *he* was the one I'd be living with. Not her.

Thumbs shaking so hard my keys are rattling, I'm all *LOL* with my own shouty caps reply, hoping she'll take them to be extra hard laughter rather than the panic-laced, not-enough-air, what-the-fuck-did-I-just-do kind of manic laughter it truly is.

How is this happening? I'm the girl who gets shit

done, on time, every time. I'm the one others turn to in a pinch. I'm *not* the girl who lands herself in an apartment with a guy she traded V-Cards with after prom... for God only knows how long.

Ugh.

Until two days ago, everything was on track. I'd handed off all my projects in Denver. I'd closed out my apartment, donated my furniture and housewares, and turned in my keys before flying home to see my dad while my clothing and personal items were shipped to the apartment GHW had lined up for me.

And then I got the email.

A pipe burst and my should-have-been apartment was unlivable for the foreseeable future. HR had no place to put me, and unless I could figure something out myself, my start date would be pushed back three weeks.

After an indulgent moment of hyperventilating, not too far off from this one, I emailed back, letting them know I'd be starting *on time*. Because that is the kind of employee I am. And then I'd whirled into action, putting out an *ask* for friends of friends living in Chicago looking for a roommate. Somehow I got to Piper, and for a minute, I thought everything had fallen into place.

Wrong.

Because there is no freaking way I can live with Ben.

I hiccup and, sucking another shaky breath, tell myself to get it together. I can turn this around. It's what

I do. I just need to get the heck out of here, find some coffee shop to message him that I've found another place but thank you, etc., etc., etc.... wait for the thumbs-up emoji of neutral acknowledgment, and then go max out my credit card on a hotel for two weeks.

Which is not how I roll.

I don't carry debt. I don't live beyond my means. And I never leave myself in a position where I don't have a bed to sleep in at night.

Call it a carryover from middle school when my family hit a rough patch and we spent two weeks living in the back of our minivan. That stuff sticks with a girl... even when it's a million miles behind her.

That said, if ever there was an emergency that justi-fied financial recklessness, this is it.

Grabbing my bag, I start back down the hall and—

"Change of heart, roomie?"

I freeze where I am. Then, head dropping, turn back to the now open doorway, and the one guy I kind of hoped I'd never have to see again standing in it.

Filling it.

To capacity.

Oomph. The sight of Ben Boerboom in the flesh knocks the air right out of me.

He's big. Bigger than I remember. Hard cut from head to toe, muscles upon muscles stacked and bulging beneath the stretch of his tight white T-shirt and worn jeans that hug his massive thighs.

His mouth is hooked in a version of the same slanted smirk I saw every day back in high school. Only it's not quite the same. Like the rest of him, it looks harder. Less invitation to mischief and more... guarded. Accusing, maybe. Or maybe that's just my own guilt talking, and all I'm seeing is indifference where it never existed before.

"Boomer." I shake my head with a sigh. "I apologize. This was a total misunderstanding. I thought—"

"That you were moving in with Piper?" He raises a brow, blond and thick with the smallest gap where he got stitches in the tenth grade.

"She texted?"

Uncrossing his arms, he pulls his phone from his back pocket. It vibrates in his hand. Then again, and before it's even through, again and again.

My brow lifts with his, and for a second, his smile feels more like the one I knew.

"Started about five minutes ago. Hasn't stopped."

Uh-huh. Okay.

"You knew I was here." I can feel the heat creeping up my neck and into my face.

"Had an apple while I watched through the door. Actually, I had two. The second was supposed to be for you. Like a 'welcome to the apartment' apple. But then you just stood there with this horror-stricken look on your face." He shrugs, those intense blue eyes never leaving mine. "So I ate it."

A choked laugh slips free, because even though I can see he isn't charmed by this whole situation... I also see a glimpse of the ridiculous guy I was half in love with from the first time he tugged my ponytail in bio to ask if he could cheat off me on the quiz... then winked, telling me he'd eaten his Wheaties *and* his Ritalin that morning, and he'd nail it on his own.

How am I actually standing face-to-face with Ben Boerboom? "No apple for me, then?"

The corner of his mouth hitches impossibly higher and he repockets his still ringing phone. "Not unless you come in. Which I can see wasn't your plan. But FYI, there are more inside."

"You were actually *okay* with me living here?" *With him?*

"I bought you a whole damn bowl of apples, didn't I?"

And then he'd watched me flip out and try to sneak off. "Boomer, I feel like a jackass here."

One eye squints. "For trying to bail without a word? Yeah, that tracks."

"That too. But... I honestly had no idea this was your apartment. And to show up here without so much as—"

"A Facebook poke?"

Another laugh escapes, and I nod. "Yeah, or anything else."

Like even a hello... in eight years. Not that he'd been sending Christmas cards either.

"Look, it's fine. Did I think it was weird as fuck that you were planning to move in without contacting me? Yeah. But now that we've cleared that up, how about you come in. Sit down while you figure out what you want to do."

I'm already nodding and, when he flashes me a grin that is so purely the guy I secretly loved from high school, it knocks the air right out of me.

"*Ben.*"

He takes my bag and winks. "Move it, Elliot."

Why not.

I'll have an apple. Book my hotel and then get the hell out.

2

Ben

The gym is my special place.

It's where I go to channel my excess energy. Sometimes it's where I try to quiet my brain, letting go of my spinning thoughts and just sinking into the push and pull of my muscles working to make me better at my job.

And sometimes it's my sucky attempt to escape whatever stupid shit I've gotten myself into.

Like a new roommate.

All I had to do was *not* open the door last night.

She would have left. I'd have gotten a text letting me off the hook. This whole mess would be filed as a near miss, and I'd be lined up to lord this thing over my sister for the next thirty years.

If I hadn't opened the door.

I wasn't going to. I'd stood there, crunching away on a Honeycrisp with Lara's name on it, staring through that fisheye lens as I cataloged surface-level changes between the woman on the other side and the eighteen-year-old girl she was the last time we were together.

Those golden, windblown waves that hung wild around her face were now tamed into a smooth, controlled fall. The cut-offs and oversized shirts that somehow always had a smudge of dirt or paint on them had been replaced by wide-legged trousers and a silk blouse in shades of cream. And instead of the Converse sneakers she'd scour the secondhand stores for, she was wearing a pair of killer heels that had me mentally screaming, *Imposter!*

I was practically holding my breath, waiting for her to leave. It's what I wanted. At least until I saw that single assertive nod she gave to herself as she grabbed her bag and turned to *actually* go.

Next thing, the door was open, and I was giving her a hard time, telling her to come inside. Chatting her up while I casually sprinkled roommate bait throughout our brief interaction.

Didn't Piper mention the housekeeper and grocery shopper?

What. The. Fuck. Boomer.

I didn't *want* Lara to move in. But apparently, my needy-as-fuck inner psyche had had enough of people skipping out on me this week and wouldn't let her do it too.

I'm gone more than I'm here, so you'd almost have the place to yourself.

That's what sealed the deal, my not being around. Figures.

Anyway, we're roommates now.

The screen on my phone blinks awake with an incoming video call from Bowie.

I drop my weights with a hard exhale and swipe to answer.

"How's Italy?"

"Gorgeous. Hot. Your sister loves it."

She's been blowing up my phone with pictures since about two a.m.

"So how is it seeing Lara again?" In the small screen, Bowie walks over to a rack and starts making his selections. "Been a minute, yeah?"

A minute. Eight years. Whatever.

"It's weird. Nice. I mean, you remember what she was like in high school."

He grins, knocking out a few squats. "Pretty. Funny. Sweet."

My brows pull together.

"Settle, Boomer. I'm not mentally stepping out on your sister so put your scowl away. I was never into Lara, but objectively speaking, she was a babe."

He's not wrong. Objectively speaking, Lara was

always hot. Confident, kind, and driven. She could talk smack and take it right back with a laugh that pulled everyone in on whatever the joke was. People were always drawn to her. Half the guys at school and more than a few of the girls were into her.

"Yeah, she's still pretty." Understatement. "That's the same." Like her laugh. Her smile. And that thing where she pushes her hair back behind her ear when she's nervous.

Same, same, same.

The way I try not to get caught up in all of the above.

Same.

I grab my bar, adjusting my grip before starting to knock out reps.

"But?"

I make a show of focusing on finishing the set then drop my weights and straighten up, rubbing my hands. "But it's been eight years. She's *not* the same." And hell, I'm not either. "So, yeah, weird."

Bowie grunts. He gets it. As much as he can, considering he was a grade ahead of us and wasn't around for that last year of high school. Or the summer after.

I move over to an open area and, propping the phone beside me, get on the floor to stretch out. Even after months of PT and healing, there's a twinge that wasn't there before my surgeries last season. According to Doc, it's to be expected and nothing to worry about. It doesn't get in the way on the ice but still catches me off guard when I move certain ways. I don't like it. I don't like any reminder of how precarious my career is— My security. Future. Life plans. But focusing on Bowie's barrage of questions about Lara isn't any better.

He rattles off one question after the next, and I sound like some reel on a loop. "Don't know, man."

He stares. "What the fuck, Boomer? You didn't ask about her family, the job that brought her to Chicago, or whether she's been in touch with any other classmates? You even bother to say hello?"

I switch legs, pulling my chest toward the floor. "Fuck off. She was freaking out, not sure about staying at all."

Same as I should have been, but no. I had to convince her what a great idea her moving in was, how it would work out for both of us. And when she finally met my eyes and asked if I really didn't mind? The level of relief I felt was... well, a little fucking alarming.

"But then she did agree," he says, giving me one of those pointed looks that is clearly a prompt for more info.

"And I didn't want to overwhelm her. Figured less was more." Sounds totally rational when I say it now.

"Less is more?" Bowie's brows pull together over confused eyes. "What does that even look like from you?"

I flip him off. "It looks like me telling her to make herself at home and then making good on the part where I promised that I was gone more than I was there. Met Tyrell out for *tapas* at that new Spanish place he's had a hard-on for since he found out who they hired as head chef."

Bowie blinks. "You and Ty tried the new Spanish place without me?"

I sigh, going for another deep stretch and ignoring the twinge near Lefty. "You moved into your new place without *me*, didn't you?"

He grunts again, this one signaling the back-off I hoped it would.

There are things between Lara and me I need to figure out. Shit no one knows about. Not Bowie, not Piper. No one... Okay, no one except my mom, but April Boerboom is a saint *and* a vault.

And until I do figure it out, I don't need my former Ride or Die asking a million questions.

But speaking of questions... "Bowie, dude, I need the name of that cleaning service you hired. Not the one that hates me. And not the one with the girl I did before I knew she was working for us either. And I need a grocery shopper too."

Lara

LAST NIGHT, it all seemed so reasonable.

I was already at the apartment. Piper had made up the room she and Bowie used to occupy with new bedding for me. Hotels were expensive as hell. And my biggest concern about connecting with Piper— her brother —turned out to be a non-issue. The guy was completely indifferent to whatever I decided.

He was indifferent to me.

There was no awkward silence. No questions. Just the offer of an organic apple and the unoccupied room in an apartment he apparently spends next to no time in.

It would have been nuts to turn down over a past with a player who's been so deep in puck bunnies for the last eight years, Piper probably had to remind him who I was.

So I thanked him as profusely as possible while he nodded, grabbed his keys off the catch-all by the door, and took off for the night. Probably a date. Hookup. Whatever it was, he didn't tell me. The days of being this guy's confidante are long over.

This morning though, I'm trying to hold on to that reasonable feeling as I sit at the table that feels like more than a breakfast nook and less than a dining-room fixture, laptop open to redirect my shipment from Denver.

The front door opens loudly, and Ben comes in, belting out a Taylor Swift song. His blond hair is sticking up in twelve directions, his heavy cheekbones wearing the evidence of time in the sun as he breaks out some dance move a guy his size shouldn't be good at.

It's so Ben, all I can do is smile as he drops his gym bag by the door. But then his eyes come up and land on me with a start.

That's right. The girl you invited to move in is actually here. Sorry!

"Morning, Boomer."

He gives me a half wave and a stiff smile, then picks up the bag he just dropped and takes it to his room without another word.

Gah. I look down at the confirmation window displayed on my screen and sigh.

Please, don't let this be a mistake.

I'm gathering up my laptop to clear out of the communal space when—

"Hey," Ben says with a jut of his chin. Because he's back.

His hands are stuffed in the pockets of his shorts, and his gray T-shirt is molded over the slopes of his hunched shoulders as he stands at the mouth of the hallway.

This is what second thoughts look like.

Sucking a shallow breath, I smile. "What's up?"

The muscle in his square-cut jaw bunches, releases. Repeats. "How's your family?"

Ben

THERE'S ALWAYS someone at the arena. Security, the cleaning crew. Once I showed up at two a.m. to clear my head and found our travel coordinator surrounded by a dozen empty coffee cups because of a snafu with a coming road trip.

This morning it feels like a ghost town. I can hear the echo of voices from within the depths of the place, disembodied laughter here and there, but aside from the guard who waved me through without a word, the place is empty.

Perfect. That's what I want.

Some quality alone time.

Just me and my thoughts.

Allll by myself.

I push into the weight room and just stand there, taking in the too-full racks, hauntingly empty benches, and neatly stacked mats with a scowl. This place is better with my team in it.

Fuck.

I'm debating whether I ought to turn my ass around and go home when—

"Yo, Boomer."

A massive mitt grips my shoulder, and I jump so high, I'm surprised I don't end up with another batch of plaster in my hair.

"You comin' or goin'?"

Clutching my chest like my mom watching *Stranger Things*, I gape at my teammate and last person I want to see. "Jesus, Static. You scared the piss out of me."

Another reason to hate all over him.

"Glad you're here actually."

I lift a skeptical brow. "That right?"

"Figured now that Baby Boomer is getting serious with Bowie, might be time for you and me to clear the air, yeah?"

I grunt. Translation: No.

"Come on, man." He steps in beside me. "You can't hold her against me forever. Nothing even happened between us, and you're still freezing me out. Meanwhile, you already forgave Bowie when he's actually—" The guy makes a series of suggestive hand gestures. "Every night."

I stop and turn to him, genuinely curious. "Do you *want* to deep-throat my fist? 'Cause it kind of seems"— I mimic the gestures —"like you might."

His head drops back, giving up an exasperated groan. "Forgive and forget. Ever heard of it?"

"Matter of fact, I have." It's something new I'm working on. "Unfortunately, I exhausted my newfound powers of forgiveness on my best friend. Fresh out for the teammate busted ogling my sister's ass."

He rolls his eyes and crosses to a treadmill. "Fine. What's got you in here so early anyway? Kitchen isn't even running yet."

I hop on the treadmill beside him. "Just clearing my head."

We start jogging at a chill pace to warm up, but it's not enough. I'm still wound tight. Still thinking about Lara. Thinking about high school. Exes and friends. Plans and pacts. How many things I had wrong back then. The things I thought I had right.

I've got to stop.

I look over to where Static is bumping up the pace. Matching it on my machine, I try to loosen up my stride, my shoulders.

No good.

He looks over and shakes his head. "All that huffing with the deep sighs over there and you've barely even started to run. Come on, man, talk. You obviously need to."

Dude is the dead last guy I'm going to share my deepest, darkest secrets with. The last.

I open my mouth to tell him that and, "It's Lara. Old friend from high school."

"Yeah, I heard. She just moved in."

Bunch of gossips, this team. Whatever. "I'm all fucked-up in the feels having her in the apartment. Because it's not just the apartment. It's not the physical space that she's occupying, you know what I mean?"

I see his mouth open in my peripheral, but again, I open mine and the fucking firehose of pent-up touchy-feely bullshit blasts free. "She's in my thoughts"— in my head and my chest —"dragging up a million memories I've tried to put to bed about how it used to be."

He hits stop on his machine, and I crank mine up.

"Wait, you guys were together, together? Swear Bowie said you were just friends."

I cut him a lethal look. "Cone of silence, Static. Pre-dawn gym is a sacred space. You think I was pissed about Piper—"

"For the millionth time, *I'm sorry*. Nothing happened with Piper."

My eyes narrow. "Uh-huh."

"But I won't say anything. Trust me."

Those two fucking words. Feels like every person who's ever uttered them to me has backtracked, found a loophole, or flat-out fed me bullshit.

Those two words are my biggest red flags. But in this moment, my need to process exceeds my need to protect myself from another "friend" fucking me over.

"She and I were just friends for almost all of high school. But there was a small window after, when that *just* was more of a *plus*." Jesus, it feels good to say out loud. To stop pretending this beast of a thing doesn't exist. "We didn't want anyone to know, make assumptions, or offer opinions."

I wanted to keep it as my own. Protect it until it had a chance to grow. Not that it ever did.

"Okay, yeah, I get that." He looks off into the resistance bands, nodding in a way that suggests he actually might. He looks back. "So, what happened?"

"We agreed before it even started it wouldn't change things. But it did. Or it did for me." I huff a breath, flashes of the way she melted into my arms and sighed my name rolling through my mind faster than the belt rolling beneath my feet.

"Not for her, I guess."

"Nope. And the thing about it... I *know* she wasn't trying to be careless with my feelings. She's not that kind of person. I think she just really saw that situation different than I did." Wasn't there when I came back from camp. Didn't come home before I had to leave again. "Fell out of touch faster than I could believe for what I thought we meant to each other. Even before the *plus* stuff, you know?"

His jaw shifts. "And now she's back. In your apartment."

"Yep."

"And you still want her."

"Yes and no. I mean, that feeling inside me from the first time, it's there." It's trying to sneak past my defenses and reach out, to connect again. But defense is kinda my thing these days.

I hit Stop and coast off the machine. "Rationally, though? I really fucking don't, because I've been down that road before... and it's a dead end."

Arms crossed over his big-ass chest, Static gives me a

thoughtful look. "I'll be honest, this isn't a conversation I expected to have with you."

I grunt, staring at my shoes a beat. "You're back in the trust tree, so I guess we're friends again. Don't fuck it up."

3

———

Lara

For a minute that first morning, I thought *maybe*. Maybe things could go back to some semblance of what they were. But every time I think I catch a glimpse of the Ben I used to know, in the next blink, he's gone. Replaced by this generous, painfully attractive, confusingly reserved version of my old friend. And my heart sinks a little lower.

The next week is a blur of overly polite, desperately superficial interactions.

How was your day?

Good. Yours?

Great.

Terrific.

We barely skim the surface of superficial, and it's awful.

How's the workout?

Good. How's the new office?

Great.

Terrific.

We keep an unnatural distance between us.

If I'm on the couch when he gets back from wherever he goes— and he's always going somewhere —it's not enough to sit on the other end or in one of the deep cushy chairs on either side. No. He stands at the far corner of the room, making sure to ask me something, anything... even if it feels like nothing.

If he's getting food in the kitchen when I'm on my way to fill up my water bottle, I linger just beyond the cutout doorway.

Which makes no sense. This kitchen is not small.

And God help us when we end up checking the mailbox at the same time or worse, have to share the elevator.

It's like this negative pressure exists between us in a way it never did when we were in high school. Not even when we were dating other people and, out of respect for those relationships, making a point not to get too close.

Now? We're both being weird when we used to just click.

It's miserable. And while I might have this kind of *awkward* coming for moving in like this, Ben definitely deserves better. So today I'm going to give it to him.

Ben

MY BRAIN IS BOUNCING HARD this morning, offering me a whole hell of a lot of opinions about the girl I moved into Bowie's room last week:

Big mistake, dude.

No, it's fine.

We should be friendlier than we are.

Eff that, keep the distance.

Does she still stay up talking halfway through the night? With who?

She looks the same.

She's not the same.

That laugh. Dude, don't get caught up in that laugh.

All reasonable enough.

And it would be one thing if my brain was the only one chiming in, but guess who finally lifted his head after six months of apathy and slumber?

Big Ben is *awake*, and ill-mannered fucker that he is, having a stretch in Lara's direction. Trying to elbow past me because "they're old friends."

As if I could forget.

Shit, if only I could forget.

So I'm trying to drain this tank of restless energy by knocking out a run on the Lakefront Trail. Usually the motion and exertion do the trick, letting my jumbled thoughts drop into place. But even with my feet hitting the path in a steady rhythm I feel through the whole of me, I can't chill.

I cut down around Burnham Harbor, checking out the boats and the people.

Lara looked pretty when she came home last night.

Bad, brain. No!

She'd been out with her new marketing team, I think. Her suit was pale blue, and her hair had come down over the course of the day. There were even a few rebel spirals around her face reminding me of the way she used to look on those humid summer nights when it was just the two of us and—

Okay, I'm not going there. Obviously.

I keep running, coming up on the Firefighter's Memorial and then the bird sanctuary where I loop back.

I wonder what she's doing today? If anyone at work has offered to show her around the city. Probably a dozen dudes, a dozen times over. And even if they haven't, she sure as hell doesn't need me to do it.

I don't even want to.

I don't.

So fucking stop thinking about her.

Running. Running. Running—

"Hey, Boomer," comes a feminine voice from the path ahead.

There are a couple twenty-something girls jogging my way. Both have banging bodies and a photoshopped kind of beauty that's generally worked for me in the past. I wait for my dick to jump, for my attention to stick, but... nothing.

"Missed you during playoffs," the redhead sings out.

Her friend giggles and adds, "She really did. You're her favorite Slayer."

I fire up the smile and thank them as I pass. Fans are great. Especially hot ones that I really ought to be thinking about getting with. Even if I'm not.

Then from behind me, Red calls, "If you ever want a running buddy... I like it hard and fast."

I look over my shoulder in time to see her friend gasp.

Red winks. "Running. And you know... other things too."

Bold.

But not even close to as bold as some of the propositions I've gotten.

Last year I'd have been jogging circles around them by now. Backwards. I'd have their digits and a plan to meet up. Hell, I might even have said screw the run and ordered a Lyft to get the three of us somewhere private.

Now?

I sure as shit could use the distraction.

I turn back, and Red's face lights up as she slows to a stop.

4

Lara

I regret all my life choices.

Or at least the ones from the last two hours, because *damn*.

I just wanted to do something nice for Ben. With that persistent strain in the air, the guy has to be regretting *his* choice to let me move in. So soft pretzels with cheese sauce. He always loved when my mom made them, and I figured I'd give her recipe a go.

What I didn't take into account was that I haven't actually made these in eight years. And even then, I probably spent more time sitting on the stool at the counter than actually *helping*. Add to that, the appliances in this kitchen are gleaming and have the look of being mostly unused.

They are in a different league than the appliances of my youth. A more powerful league... with the kind of dough-flinging reach I suspect we'll be finding evidence of for weeks.

But my most immediate problem isn't that drying glob splattered against the window in the next room. It isn't the sink full of soaking mixing bowls, measuring cups, and pans. It's not even the Lara-sized outline of flour coating the cabinets opposite the standing mixer.

No, it's that while I was trying to rinse some pretzel dough out of my hair, I somehow got a section caught around the faucet... and I've been trapped, bent over the sink, trying to escape it for five minutes already. And I really, really don't want Ben coming home to this train wreck in action.

Another futile attempt at blindly extracting myself from the faucet, and it's time to consider those kitchen shears on the counter behind me. I can't reach with my hands... but maybe my foot?

I stretch out my leg like some amateur contortionist, toes feeling around when—

"*Whoa*, Lara, what the— Are you okay?"

My eyes snap to where Ben's rubbing his jaw in the doorway as he takes in his kitchen and me. I pull my leg back and swear a silent oath never to leave my bedroom in pajamas again. Because yeah, that too.

"Heya, Boomer," I greet, all casual, like my right boob isn't submerged in a sink full of soapy dishwater and my back isn't about to go into spasm from being stuck like this. "Made you breakfast."

"Breakfast... and a show?"

Hmm. "You're hilarious."

Still, I've got to give it to the guy, he doesn't miss a beat. He mutters a quiet, "Elle," and moves to my side, the careful pressure at my scalp telling me he's working on the knot.

"How was the workout?" I ask, hoping he'll ignore the uneven tone.

He grunts, leaning closer, his torso brushing the bare skin of my arm and causing an inadvertent gasp to sneak past my lips. Because I can feel the stacks of his abs *with my elbow*.

"Sorry," he mutters, trying keep a sliver of space between us while bending over the sink with me.

"It's okay." I wait for him to ask just what in holy hell happened here, but he doesn't. Two tugs and a bit of swearing later, I'm free.

I straighten with a moan as my muscles adjust. And then, overwhelmed by gratitude and relief, I throw my arms around the big sweaty giant. "*My hero!* Thank you, thankyouthankyou!"

This guy used to give the most incredible hugs. The kind where his arms wrapped all the way around you. And just when you thought it couldn't get any better than the warmth of his body and the feel of being enveloped in that oversized hold, he'd pull you in just a little tighter.

They were the best.

But now? Ben doesn't return the hug, instead clearing his throat as he takes a step back. His eyes go to the ceiling, the window... the floor?

Anywhere but me.

It's only when the cool air and damp clothing combine that I look down and—

"Ack!" My arms fly across my chest, and a shocked laugh bursts free. Because yep, there's my nipple peeking through the pink polka-dot fabric of my PJs that, at this point, are essentially transparent.

Ben's eyes snap to mine, twitch, and dip again.

"Fuck," he hisses, eyes returning to the ceiling once more. There's a dishrag at the side of the sink, and he blindly grabs it, though I'm not sure for what. To wash out his eyes maybe.

Except point two seconds later... It hits me.

With a splat.

Straight in the face.

Sputtering, I squint through one eye as he holds his hand in front of him, trying to blot out the view of my body.

"Go change, Elliot. Right this fucking minute." His face is red. His ears are red. And he's chanting "Don't look" again and again... *while looking*.

And I'm trying to leave. I *want* to.

I actually make it a few steps before I glance down at

the dripping wet, seven-inch-square towel in my hands and crack, because... really?

"Stop laughing," he begs, only at this point he's laughing too. Laughing, still holding his hand up between us while I collapse in the doorway, using my arm to block my boobs.

Lifting the rag with my free hand, I try to keep a straight face. "What is *this*?"

"I was trying *to help*," he argues back, trying for indignant.

"It hit me *in the face*!" And now the moment has well and truly gotten away from me, like I'm laughing so hard there are tears.

I fling it back, aiming for his neck, but this is Ben Boerboom, one of the top defenders in the NHL, and he catches it out of the air before it even gets close.

It's hilarious. It's mightily hot too, not that I should notice.

The oven timer dings, and I perk up. This is my moment.

Scrambling to my feet, I grab the hot pads and give Ben my most winning smile. This is going to knock his sporty ankle-cut socks off. "I made you pretzels."

And oh my God, the look on his face.

"Your mom's?" At my nod, he completely forgets about my boobs. "Get 'em out, get 'em out."

I give him a hip-check and bend down to open the oven—

"Mother*fucker*."

～

Ben

"BOOMER, *please*. You don't have to eat them."

Lara is hovering, closer than she's been since she moved in, those big brown eyes a mix of disappointment and frustration as I force my teeth through the abomination in my mouth.

Maybe I should have taken Red up on her offer instead of taking a picture with her before heading back. But even as I think it, I know I wouldn't have. I wasn't interested in those girls on the path, no-strings distraction or not.

"S'good." I'm nodding, trying to hide my grimace behind a grin as I chew and chew and chew— God help me —and chew. Lara lets out a huff and pushes past.

She's still wearing those little PJs, thin enough that even without being soaked when she bends over to grab the trash out of its drawer, I have to close my eyes. Not that it does much good with my mind hyper-focused on her mile-long legs and that unconventional show of flexibility I walked in on. How her nipple was bunched so tight I couldn't help but think about the feel of it pressed between my tongue and roof of my mouth. Or how having the length of her body against mine, even just for a second, was such a shock to the system, it took everything I had not to react like the last eight years haven't happened at all and just pull her in the way I used to.

Jesus, don't think about what it was like to hold her.

Except, I'm totally thinking about it...

Her back against the wall as I rocked between the legs around my hips...

Beneath me, staring up into my eyes, lips parted as I sank full-length into her snug, wet heat...

Atop my chest with her hand resting over my heart, lashes fanned shut against her cheeks as she slept...

Eject, eject, eject!

My eyes blast open, and I find Lara in front of me. She looks like the prettiest, most ridiculous drowned rat ever as she holds the bin in my face. "Spit."

She made this recipe for me. She *remembered* that I loved it.

My lips pinch shut, and I dig deep, chewing like it's my job. I'm not spitting her kindness into the trash. No way. I'm almost ready to risk the swallow, pretty sure we're past the lacerated throat stage, when Lara grabs my face with her free hand. Our eyes lock. "*Spit.*"

I've seen that not-fucking-around look before. Been on the receiving end of it enough to know she's serious. So I reluctantly do as asked, and then watch as she takes the baking sheet with the other petrified puddles of wishes-they-were-pretzels-but-OMG-no-they-fucking-aren't and dumps them as well.

Setting both aside, she leans against the counter beside me and wipes the back of her hand over her brow, smearing a bit of floury paste there instead of wiping it away.

Cute.

Messy.

Ahh, fuck it.

I grab a paper towel and run the corner under the tap. "Here, let me."

Her eyes come up, and there's a searching vulnerability in them, like maybe she's looking for the guy she used to know or something— and it hits me square in the chest. For a heartbeat, I almost want to be him.

"Sorry about the kitchen. And your teeth," she says quietly, inches separating us now instead of an entire room.

I shake my head, catching her chin in a light hold as I bring the towel to her face. "It was thoughtful. Sweet. And my teeth have taken a puck to them. They could have handled your pretzel."

Probably.

She watches me as I wipe at her brow, then down the smooth skin of her cheek. Along the delicate line of her jaw and over to that spot beneath her ear that used to make her lose her mind when I kissed it.

Back in high school, I never really let myself look at her those first years. I wouldn't risk seeing anything but the friend she was to me. Not while I was committed to someone else. But after prom, I finally let myself. And once I did, I couldn't look away.

Day after day. Night after night, I got lost in the lines of her face. The slope of her nose. The smattering of freckles... these two right here, so close they're almost touching. The fullness of her bottom lip and neat bow of her top. I memorized it all.

Over the years, I tried to forget. Failed. Found myself thinking about those two freckles and this little divot more often than I should have.

Seeing her now, *really* seeing her for the first time since she moved in, I can't deny that she's only gotten more beautiful. Her face is as hard to look away from now as it was then.

But I need to.

She bites her lip. "The pretzels were supposed to be an olive branch."

Huh.

I toss the paper towel and step back so I'm leaning against the opposite counter. "Do we need one?"

Her slender shoulder comes up, and she shakes her head. "I don't know what we need. Maybe just for me to find another place."

Wait, what?

"You're looking?" Why it surprises me, I have no idea.

"Ben, I shouldn't be here. You've been beyond generous, but you can't tell me this feels right to you."

It doesn't. But her leaving doesn't feel right either.

It feels fucking wrong. And suddenly, that jumpy tension is back under my skin.

"You don't need to find another apartment. There's plenty of space here."

"And you don't owe me any of it."

"I know I don't *owe* you. I just— *fuck*." I shove a hand through my hair and meet her eyes, letting her see the truth in mine. "I don't know how to be around you anymore."

Her head hangs low, that smile I've done crazy things to earn nowhere to be seen. And I hate myself for being the reason it's gone.

I need to knock my shit off and fix this. "Hey, I don't want you to leave."

"Really?"

She won't even look at me.

Maybe I wasn't sure before, but I am now. "Yeah."

Lara worries her lip between her teeth. "Okay. I'm taking you at your word about the apartment. Thank you. But if you change your mind, you'll let me know. And even if you don't, I don't expect— I— We don't have to be friends."

Ooph.

The words hit like a blow. Harder than they should after all this time. I turn them over once more. It's enough.

"Here's the thing, Elliot." I scrub my jaw. "Our

baggage is from a million years ago. Sure, we crossed some lines, had some fun... A *lot* of fun."

Her lips part in surprise.

Yeah, didn't see myself going *there* either. But this needs to be said.

"We were young. Headed in different directions. College. The league. Life happened and we drifted apart. That's all."

It wasn't her fault that I'd quietly gotten it in my head we might be more. Or that when I realized *more* wasn't in the cards for us and she was moving on with her life exactly the way we promised each other we would, I couldn't handle it. That when the time and distance started to grow, it was easier to let it build and build... until that's all there was.

It wasn't her fault. And it wasn't totally mine. Which I'm feeling mature AF being able to acknowledge.

It's kind of freeing, actually.

I reach out and take her hand. "But before all that? We were really, *really* good friends."

Her eyes meet mine. "Yeah, we were. The best."

I nod. "I *miss* being friends with you."

"I miss it too."

Damn, there's that smile again. A little bittersweet. A little hopeful.

I shrug. "So maybe we give it a shot. See if there's a way we can get some of that back?"

I'm not sure I'll ever be able to look at her without

seeing all the stuff that's about being *more* than friends. But even though it's there, might always be there... That line between friendship and *more* is not one I'll cross again.

"Yes." Her grin is as bright as the sun. "I'd like that a lot."

~

Lara

FRIENDS. My heart is racing.

We're smiling at each other now, eyes locked for what's maybe longer than they should be, but for once it just feels right. Easy. Almost like it used to.

Is that even possible? That maybe we could actually get back to—

"Hello, hello!" comes a singsong greeting from the front of the apartment.

"Expecting company?" I ask as Ben breaks the eye contact to groan into his fist.

We haven't really talked about dates or dating, so I have no idea if he's got a girl with a key, or based on the rumors, a lot of girls with keys.

In answer, he pushes off the counter and strides out of the kitchen, bellowing along the way, "Nope! Uh-uh. Piper, your key privileges are revoked. Unless you dumped Bowie's ass. No. Even then. You can stay with Mom and Dad. I get Bowie in the divorce."

"Shut it, Ben." She laughs warmly as I'm stepping out of the kitchen.

And this gorgeous woman who I can't quite wrap my head around being little Piper Boerboom is standing there. Whoa. With Grant Bowie's hands resting possessively on her shoulders.

Craziness! "I know you told me you were together, but seeing it? Oh my God!"

I turn to Ben, who was always *so* protective of his little sister. At least back in high school. "For real, I'm stunned you didn't lose your mind over them dating."

Two sets of eyes skirt away and one hits the ceiling. And I cough out a laugh because clearly, he did.

Then Piper breaks away from Grant with a bounce and a squeal and, completely ignoring my current baking trainwreck status, pulls me in tight as the guys do the bro-hug, busting knuckles thing. "Lara, I'm *so* glad you're still here, and I'm so sorry about the mix-up! With our moving and leaving town all at once, it was just— gahh. Forgive me?"

"Please. You guys saved me. I was in a bad spot with my apartment falling through."

Piper sighs, pulling me in again. "Girl, I have been there. I'm just glad it worked out."

When Piper lets me go, Bowie's next, giving me a hug that takes me right off my feet. "Good to see you,

Elliot. Surviving life with Boomer?" He puts me down and looks me over. "I'm afraid to ask what happened here."

"Kitchen snafu," I say, feeling around my hair for any stray pretzel dough.

But then Ben's at my side, fingers sifting gently through my hair, body close enough that I can feel the heat coming off him as he picks out a sizeable glob.

"I gotchu," he says with a quiet smirk that throws me back through the years to that time when we were a team. When there was us, and there was everyone else.

I know it won't be like that again. Not really.

But in this moment, it feels like it is, and... and I like it probably more than I should.

Ben

LARA DUCKS back to her room to clean up while my sister brushes a bit of flour from her shirt before flinging herself onto the couch. Bowie moves in beside her, pulling her feet into his lap.

Gross.

I mean *great.* Love how nauseatingly in love my little sister and former— *fuck* —I mean eternal best friend are.

Love. It.

46

I smile. Tightly.

They grin.

I roll my eyes. Piper forgets I'm there and pokes Bowie's ribs with her toes, eliciting a low growl that is going to haunt my fucking nightmares, it's so far past the PG-13 rule we had in place while they lived here.

I huff. They ignore me, murmuring to each other.

"So how was the trip?" I ask desperately.

"Amazing," they say in unison, threading their fingers together.

Bare fingers. Still no rings, so that referenced "amazing" can only mean one thing. And I don't want to think about it. "And the new apartment? You guys enjoying the place?"

The look they give each other is completely uncalled for, and the gag reflex is real. Not that they notice.

"*Hello?* What am I, invisible here? My house, my rules. No eye-fucking my little sister in front of me, dude!"

Bowie takes his sweet time tearing his attention from Piper, but then gives me a legit apologetic shrug before changing the subject. "You and Elliot seem to have fallen back into that old groove."

I look down the hall toward her closed door and nod. "Yeah, getting there. Like I told you the other day, it was a little stiff at first."

He lifts a brow, and I wave him off. "Not like that, dick."

"Hey, you said *stiff*. We've met." He gives up a gruff laugh. "Not sure how else I was supposed to take it."

"Oh, come on." Piper gives him another toe to the ribs. "You know that's not how it is with them."

"It's not how it *was* with them," he corrects, catching her foot to— oh hell no —bite the side. "But our man here isn't exactly the same kid he was back when he was saving himself for love and marriage."

"Guys, I'm right here." When did I become the most ignorable guy in the room?

Piper sighs. "I am aware of his fuck-boy status. He might be banging half of Chicago, but *not* Lara Elliot."

Bowie lifts a brow half a millimeter, all, *You sure about that?*

Piper snorts.

I look down the hall again. Door still closed. But it won't be for long, and this is not a discussion I want overheard. "Yo. Cut it out."

Do they listen? No.

"Sweetheart, eight years is a long time. With Boomer, eight hours is—"

"*Enough*," I snap, startling them both. My heart is pounding harder than it should be, and I'm half out of my chair. "Eight years *is* a long time, and while Lara and I were tight in high school, this roommate situation is new. So I'd really fucking appreciate it if you didn't make her uncomfortable with all your speculation. Fair?"

Chastened, they both nod.

Then, less than a second later, Piper bounces in her seat and stage-whispers to Bowie, "But you know I'm right."

She's beaming when she turns back to me. "Come on. Admit it. You love me for finding you the perfect replacement roommate. Say it."

She looks so hopeful I forgive her all over again. I'm getting scary good at this being-the-bigger-person shit. "Yeah, yeah. I love you, sis."

I'm thinking maybe Bowie's going to chime in, beg for me to reaffirm our BFF status next, but instead he seems to be surveying the apartment, a furrow digging between his brows.

"Aside from the kitchen, this place looks pretty good." Eyes narrowed, he turns to me. "*Too good*. If you're making Lara pick up after your filthy ass—"

"Who, me?" she asks, emerging from the back hall with a wide smile, damp hair thrown up in a messy knot and wearing a pair of new athletic shorts and an old T-shirt from our high school that's threadbare in a few places.

She looks so much like the girl I used to know, I almost strain my neck doing a double take.

Which, thank you, baby Jesus, she doesn't notice.

Taking the open chair on the other side of the couch, she waves a hand around. "Nah, Boomer's got someone who cleans and shops." She turns to Bowie. "Sylvia. Same person you've had for the last year, right?

Anyway, I haven't met her yet. She comes while I'm at work."

Piper stops wiggling her toes into Bowie's side, and the perma-scowl on his face is replaced by a smooth stunned stare as they take another, slower study of the space they used to occupy with me.

Bowie's brows lift. "Sylvia. Riiight."

Piper's staring at me, wide-eyed, mouth gaping.

Christ.

"And *Sylvia* does the shopping for you guys too?" Bowie asks, leaning forward where he sits. "Same as she did when we lived here?"

I nod, firing fucking lasers through my eyes.

And because they're *them* instead of, say, me, they let it drop, take a beat, and change the subject to their trip to Italy.

But I'd bet my shitty left nut I'll be hearing about this later.

We hang out a while, but Bowie and Piper need help moving their new big-ass bedframe to the opposite wall in their bedroom. Because, of course they do.

Couldn't be the fridge or some unwieldy entertainment center.

Nope. *Their* bed. In their bedroom.

Whatever.

I head up to their place... which is literally the apartment above ours, avoid looking at anything in their shared space while Bowie and I muscle the bed into three different spots before Piper taps her chin and tells us to put it back in the original spot, and then come back down to help Lara with the pretzels-gone-wrong flour explosion.

When I get to the kitchen, she's standing tiptoe on a stool, wiping down the light fixtures.

"Whoa, easy up there," I say, and a few things hit me in rapid succession.

First, apparently, I'm hardwired to keep this woman safe, because I'm at her side in a blink, steadying her with one hand at her hip while doing my best goalie impression— arm out, shifting up and down, trying to anticipate any weak spot that needs protecting —with the other. This girl is not going down.

Second, if we're *really* going to be friends, the wayward thoughts need to stop. Which means, after I'm sure Lara isn't in jeopardy of breaking her neck, the "no touching rule" circa sophomore year is back in effect.

It worked then. It'll work now.

Third and last, *Sylvia* wouldn't even *think* to wipe down the lights.

Lara chuckles. "Almost done."

"Sorry, I was going to help clean up." Another reason to resent the trip upstairs.

"Seriously, that mess was all me. And it didn't take too long." She swipes the rag over one last bit of glass. "There. Like it never happened."

I nod as she reaches for my shoulder. Then with as

much clinical detachment as I can muster, help her back to the floor.

My hands are off her almost as fast as they were on.

She gives me a warm smile and sweeps her phone off the counter on her way out.

Part of me wants to follow, hang out some more. Because it feels like a wall came down between us, and now that it has, the teenager in me is dying for more of his favorite buddy. But I don't want to push too hard too fast. Friendships aren't rebuilt in a day. So I keep my feet glued in place, contemplating if ten seconds is enough figurative space before I leave too, or if I should give it thirty.

"Hey, Boomer?"

My head snaps up to where Lara is back, swinging through the cutout doorway like her hand is a hinge.

I can feel my fucking ears turning red, being busted loitering like a weirdo. But I fake like I'm cool. Ish.

Chin jut. Smirk. "S'up?"

S'up? New low achieved.

She knows it. I know it.

But damn, I love that telltale flicker at the corner of her mouth. She bites her lip, and I tell myself to look away, but I don't. I fucking can't.

"Some friends from work were telling me about this fair going on this weekend. Taste of Lincoln Avenue, I think?"

"Yeah, it's awesome." My favorite thing about staying

in Chicago in the off-season is the summer festivals. "Like a huge street party. Food. Bands. It's cool. You should check it out."

She nods, lifting a slim shoulder. "Want to go?"

5

———

Lara

I don't know what prompted me to invite Ben.

Or why he said yes.

Or how something I figured would be a couple hours of easygoing distraction somehow became a day-into-night, citywide tour of neighborhood street parties, live bands, whiskey tastings, beer gardens, and most recently, talking for hours in the back corner booth of Belfast Bar.

What I do know is that I can't remember having a better time... at least not in the last eight years.

And God, it feels good to laugh like this again.

Ben sits back, smiling over his beer before he takes a long swallow.

I'm momentarily distracted by the way his throat

moves up and down, how even the muscular column of his neck is attractive.

Like his big hands and the every-which-way quality of his hair.

And those little lines at the corners of his eyes that weren't there the first time I looked into them.

"So, Elliot," he starts, but then leaves me hanging until I reply, "Boomer."

The corner of his mouth twitches, just the one side. Just enough for that panty-melting dimple to wink at me.

Even the elements of his face are flirts. Given the fact that my plans, and probably his too, ensure there's no chance of anything coming of it... that flirtation is pure fun.

"Got a guy back in Denver?"

"Nope."

He waits. Blinks. And then gives me the kind of pointed look that has me wondering why I even try to resist. When this man wants information, he gets it.

Slouching into my corner of the booth, I sigh. "My position in Denver was temporary. A steppingstone. It wouldn't have made sense to start something."

"How long were you there?"

"Couple years."

He coughs, leaning forward. "And because you weren't staying, you didn't date... *at all*?"

Geez.

"No. I dated. Some. Just..." I knew I'd leave. That I *wanted* to move on. And it would be easier to go without the entanglement of a relationship.

"Juuust... Enough to scratch the itch?"

Annnd my cheeks are on fire. Who asks that?

Obviously, Ben does. Over-sharer extraordinaire. King of the inappropriate inquiries. Boundary-impaired, TMI-afflicted Ben. He's so fun.

I take another drink. Brazenly meet his eyes across the table. "Pretty much."

He blinks again. Or maybe that was a twitch, because even though he's wearing the same smirk, there's something about his eyes that suggests he wasn't expecting that answer. At least not from me.

But he recovers fast enough.

"That mean a boyfriend's off the table for the Chicago rung on your climb up the corporate ladder too?" At my nod, he goes on. "You don't get lonely?"

"Who, me?" I quirk my brow. "Never. My badass career keeps me warm at night."

He snorts, shaking his head.

"Do *you*?" I ask with a laugh.

"Pfft. Don't talk crazy."

"Okay, since you brought dating up," I start as he coughs an "uh-oh" into his hand. "By all accounts... you're pretty popular with the ladies. Or I guess, gossip is that you've got a thing for 'puck bunnies'?"

Tongue wetting his full bottom lip, he lifts a brow.

"You been keeping tabs on me, Elliot?"

"No." Maybe. A little. "But it's pretty hard to miss when my office spends most of their water-cooler time chatting about the vast and varied sex life of the *one-girl-forever-virgin* I knew back in high school."

His mouth is screwed up like he's trying to keep a straight face, but the laughter shines bright in his eyes. "That what's printed next to my yearbook picture, you think?"

"Nah. It says, 'Math Nerd.'"

"Bullshit. It says, 'Hot AF Hockey God, Lord of the Maths, Giver.'"

I choke. *"Giver?"*

"Um, yeah? Three years in a row making sure your ass didn't just limp through those AP math finals but *crushed* them."

This is totally true. I owe him my scholarships. But, "I don't know. How about, 'Goofy AF. Big for His Age. Pays His Debts'... since we both know you owed me for dragging *your* ass past the finish line in English."

He gasps, slapping a hand over his wounded heart. Next thing, he's texting his *mom*— who he swears stays up late —and she's digging out his old yearbook to send him his picture.

Whoa.

It's... not what I remembered.

And then, we're leaning over the table to meet in the middle, howling at his phone. Because not only is Ben rocking some *awful* hockey hair and a serious acne breakout, the only caption reads, "Benjamin Boerboom. No quote provided."

But the best part is his mom's accompanying text.

"Should have sprung for the retouching package."

I will never stop laughing.

"This is why she didn't update my junior year picture on the mantel. Now I get it."

Ben's *face* as he slumps back in his booth. I can't stop.

"Man, how did I think I was hot? That picture—"

He shivers.

Sighs.

And I try to resist, hold out for even a minute, but when he just sighs louder, I crack. "*Fine*, you win! This picture is a travesty. You were, without question, the most attractive guy in school. Satisfied?"

"*Were?*"

My head drops forward. When I look up, he's grinning, victorious.

We laugh, joke about bad pictures for a while, but eventually the conversation circles back to where it started. Ben and the bunnies. He isn't embarrassed, doesn't mind talking about it. Which I'm glad for because I'm not judging.

"Yeah, guess I get around." He shrugs, taps his bottle to the beat of the music. His eyes come back to mine. "I like bunnies. They're easy. Fun. Up for a good time. Know the score before they even leave for the club."

The club, the bar, the party. The parking lot after the game. Details about Chicago's naughtiest player, whispered by a coworker who has no idea who I'm living with.

"The score?"

"Yeah, that whatever happens between us—whether it's one night or a dozen —hooking up is about getting off. It's physical. Some mutual satisfaction. That's it."

"No commitments."

"Exactly. No misunderstandings. No hurt feelings. And no expectations beyond that night." He shrugs. "It's easy, and easy is all I want."

I should take what he's saying at face value.

Who am I to question him?

It's just... once upon a time, Ben Boerboom was the ultimate commitment guy. I knew him back when the only thing he wanted was to spend the rest of his life with one undeserving girl. The one I hated for breaking his heart and selfishly owed for giving me the chance to hold a piece of it for that short time.

I honestly thought he'd be married within a year of getting his first NHL contract.

Not to *me*. What happened between *us* wasn't about forever. It was a rebound. I knew it going in—

Wait.

I blink, a dawning horror building inside me.

"Boomer," I wheeze. "Was I... the *first*... bunny?"

Ben chokes on his beer. Coughs and smacks the table. Eyes watering, he shakes his head until he can breathe again. *"What?"*

"I knew the score too," I press, ticking off matching qualifiers. Physical. Mutual satisfaction. A dozen nights and no expectations.

His big hand waves between us, recapturing my attention. "Take a breath, Elliot."

I gulp air.

"Umm, that's not—" This is maybe the first time I've seen Ben truly at a loss for words. "Let me ask you this. How many of my teammates, then and now, have you hooked up with?"

"Zero."

He knows this.

A nod. "But would it have been all the same to you if it had been one of them that night... just so long as it was someone *from the team*?"

Eww.

"Okay." I sit back, settling a little. "So *not* the first bunny."

That smirk. Glad he's amused.

"Sorry, but nope. Not the first bunny..." He winks. "Just the *first*."

Ben

I SLEEP UNTIL SEVEN THIRTY. Pretty late for me, but I'm still up before Lara. Still grinning over yesterday. Last night. And the idea that had me springing out of bed when I could totally have justified another thirty minutes or so.

Whatever, I got enough sleep to last a lifetime being out last season.

I brush my teeth, pull on my running gear, and head out into the humid morning air.

My mind is as calm as it ever gets, and the sounds of my feet hitting the pavement have me drifting into a kind of Zen state. I feel good.

Good about Lara, good about my nut, good about this three-day skills camp Bowie and I signed up for in Arizona later this week. Unlike the team training camp that happens just before pre-season, this is a private thing where we'll be working on specific skills development with an elite coach and a handful of defensive guys from around the league.

It's hard work, but I'm looking forward to sharpening my edge... and seeing a few buddies from other teams in an environment where we aren't at odds.

So yeah, it's all good.

About a block from home, I pop into my favorite convenience store. The owner is this woman who's got to be seventy if she's a day, and every time she sees me, she starts chatting me up.

She knows who I am. Teased me about putting my

"big, strong hockey muscles" to good use more than once. I usually end up helping her with something heavy and getting an earful about her grandkids.

"Well, good morning, gorgeous." She puts down her copy of the *Trib* and leans both elbows on the counter, giving me a once-over that would make a mere mortal blush. "Come by to beg me to run away with you?"

"Hey, Mel. I would, but you keep turning me down."

Her lipstick is pink and kind of all over the place, no doubt thanks to her shaky hands. But at the moment, it's definitely curving up at the corners. "I like a persistent man. Proves his devotion."

"Got it. Keep trying."

I hit the coolers first, grabbing an energy drink and then a can of wannabe tea that Lara used to like back in high school. Why not, right?

I set the drinks on the counter, and she lifts a penciled brow. "You don't drink this crap."

She's right. Not even sure Lara still does, but she'll get a kick out of seeing it anyway.

"Couple more things. One sec." I find what I'm looking for in the second aisle and set them beside the drinks. "That's it."

She hums, ringing me up. "Steppin' out on me already?"

"Never. This is for a friend. That's all." It is. But the way I'm grinning, I can see why Mel doesn't buy it.

I skip the bag and make the trip home, saying hi to

the few people out this early on a Sunday morning. Lara's still sleeping when I get back, so I set my haul on the counter and pull a platter from one of the cabinets she wouldn't be able to reach without me.

Satisfied, I jump in the shower and then dress in a pair of summer-weight trousers and a shirt nice enough for a brunch meeting with my agent.

Lara's leaving her room the same time I leave mine.

"Can't believe I slept so late." She yawns with a smile.

She's got that messy bun thing going on and a wrinkle from her pillowcase across her makeup-free face. Cute.

"I can. We must have traversed the city six times yesterday."

She tips her head in agreement. "Lots to see. Lots to do."

When we get to the kitchen, I hang back at the doorway.

She ventures in with another yawn, stretching one fisted hand wide before—

She coughs out a laugh, looking back at me with an open-mouthed smile. "Boomer!"

"Made you breakfast."

She rounds the counter to where I set out the platter with a bag of pretzel rods and a jar of queso. There's also a twig I found on the sidewalk and topped with a Spanish olive, which she picks up with one hand before doubling over, holding her stomach with the other.

Damn, she's got the best laugh.

I take a picture with my phone and then pocket it as I walk in, leaning against the counter beside her. "Not quite as special as the peace offering pretzel breakfast you made for me."

"Oh my God, and you brought me an Eye-C-T too?" She holds up the can and, cheeks pink and bright, cracks it open. "This stuff is poison."

I told her that ten years ago. "You don't have to drink it. Really."

She gives me a cross between a straight-arm and clothesline, tipping the can and gulping it back like a frat boy.

Whoa, that moan.

I swallow hard and look away to give Big Ben a second to get a grip. God, he's insufferable.

When I turn back, Lara's incoming. She flings her arms around me, and mine close around her. I pull her off her feet and pop her onto the counter before there's time to get distracted by how nice she feels.

And there she sits, eating pretzels, drinking her iced tea-flavored beverage, and chatting with me about our plans for the week, for camp, and for everything else we manage to fit into the conversation before I have to go meet my agent.

Lara

BEN FLEW OUT THIS AFTERNOON, and while he told me he was gone more than not when I arrived, this is the first time he's left town since I moved in. It's not like I haven't had my share of being alone in this space, but it's strange knowing he won't be strolling around the corner at any moment, belting out some Cher song that predates his birth by a dozen years.

The guy is such a goof. So much fun. And after finding ourselves interacting in a way that feels remarkably similar to our pre-prom past together, I'm a little bummed knowing I won't be seeing him for a few days. A little bummed, and possibly a tiny bit anxious that time and space will break the spell and when he comes home it won't be the same easy joking, talking-more-every-time-our-paths-cross fun we've fallen into over the last few days.

Okay or maybe I'm overestimating the re-bonding between us.

Maybe Ben's got a million friends he clicks with this way, and I'm turning into some possessive creeper buddy.

Ugh... Maybe I shouldn't have done that thing before he left.

Closing my laptop, I walk into the kitchen and open

the cabinet where we keep the dry snacks. Stare a minute and wish for a time machine to go back and stop myself from sneaking into his room while he was packing and—

My phone vibrates, and when I check the screen, it's Ben requesting a video call.

Heart in my throat, I accept... and there he is, laughing as he holds up the bag of pretzel rods I snuck under his stack of sweat-wicking sport shirts.

Anxiety alleviated.

"Elliot, you kill me." He shakes his head, tearing open the bag to dive in.

"How's it going?"

He chews. Swallows. "Been looking forward to working with this coach for months, but when I dragged my bag into the hotel room, I just wasn't feeling it."

"What? I thought you were excited about this trip." I grab a rod same as he has.

"The training's going to be awesome." He takes another bite, twirling the rod in his fingers. "The hotel, less so. Gotten used to company in the evenings at home."

Aww, me too. "You don't think you'll be hanging out with the guys?"

"No, I will." He wags his head. "Just, not the same."

I lean back against the counter and nod. "I get it."

One brow lifts. "We talking in the kitchen again?"

I look around, realizing I've set the phone on the

windowsill behind the sink. "Of course. Catching up on the day over a shared snack."

That grin. "Our thing."

Then his big hand is coming at me, and the background swirls around before his face takes up the screen again. "Ready to have your mind blown?"

I blink because the last time he asked me that was eight years ago and under very different, very naked circumstances.

Giving myself a mental hand slap, I ground myself in the now. This call. "Ready."

He leans closer, so I'm looking at one giant eye and the crooked line of his nose. "We're in two places at once. Talking in our kitchen and kickin' back at the hotel." The screen flips, and he slowly pans around a hotel room that's nice but not nearly as nice as I imagined. "Where do you want to sit?"

"Mmm, choices, choices. How about on the table by the window."

"Nice pick," he says, moving in that direction. "Great view too."

"I meant facing you, goof."

The phone flips back, and he fills the screen, leaning close to wink. "So did I. Get another pretzel and pour a glass of that white I left you in the door of the fridge. Wanna hear how the new project's coming."

6

Ben

"**P**ick up avocados and limes for game night!!"
I grin at Lara's scribbled reminder stuck
on the mirror next to the front door on one of
the Tiny Twist shaped sticky notes I found online when
I got back from camp.

Pretzels are our thing now.

Solid choice for a second-chance friendship if you
ask me. And fun. I like pointing with the rods for
emphasis when I talk. I like snacking on them. And
there is very little in this world more hilarious than
when Lara starts nibbling the salt crystals off one at a
time. And since she seems to be on the same page, guess
what I had delivered to her office last week.

It was this whole bouquet thing. Very fancy. And the

look on her face when she walked me through the entire selection— at a whisper, because she was at work, and I was in an exam room waiting on the doc to give my problem-child nut a clean bill of health —*priceless*.

PS: Those wayward thoughts that were accosting me on the regular when she first moved in? Almost completely gone.

Grabbing my shoes, I head back to my bathroom.

Sure, every now and then— couple times a week, max —some stray thought goes barreling past the platonic line and into the DZ. The Deviant Zone. But I shut that shit down faster than it can cause an incident. Because in my hierarchy of needs, protecting this friend-ship ranks a fuck-ton higher than finding out what that stretch of skin at the curve of Lara's neck would taste like dusted with pretzel salt.

Or if I could make her moan the way she did after practically shot-gunning her imitation iced tea.

Or what it would be like to have my fingers in her hair for something other than picking out globs of drying dough... Maybe we should try to make the scratch pretzels again.

Shit.

Okay, so that's three times and it's only Wednesday, but whatever. I'm getting a handle on it, and things with Lara have never been better.

I didn't think we'd ever get back to where we were in high school, clicking so hard half the time we know

69

what the other person is thinking before they even say it, but somehow, even with all the years apart, we already are.

We talk. We text. We send silly memes and talk trash and— damn, I haven't felt like someone *got me* this way in forever. Not since the last time I felt it with her.

It's fucking amazing. And those stray thoughts? They'll be gone in no time.

Ben

"Yikes, Ben," my sister drawls, running her finger along the entertainment center a week later. "You might need to have a word with *Sylvia* about her dusting."

I set my bowl of guac on the coffee table in front of the couch with enough force a chunky green glop splatters over the side. Great. More for *Sylvia*.

"Ehh, cut her some slack, sweetheart." Bowie steps up behind Piper, wrapping his arms around her in a possessive hold that, based on that slick smirk he shoots my way, is at least seventy-five percent for my benefit. "She's trying. And yeah, she's not the best."

"Not even close," Piper agrees like our shared blood means nothing.

"Probably somewhere in the bottom fifth percentile."

Bottom fifth? "The fuck—?"

Bowie winks. "Give it a few years. Eventually she'll master the basics."

My molars grind together, and I'm about to say something I'm sure I'll regret when Lara breezes in carrying a pitcher of margaritas in one hand and a bag of limes in the other. "I think she's doing a pretty good job. But if you don't like her work, is there a reason you can't hire someone else?"

The question hangs in the air for a beat and then Piper coughs out a cackling laugh.

Bowie rubs a hand over her back. "Our man Boomer here has some issues hanging on to cleaning services."

Dick.

"Issues?" She drops onto the couch beside me with a curious look.

"I was messy."

Piper snorts. "Messy like he can't keep his dick in his pants and his crap off the floor. Although it looks like he's gotten better about that second part. But the first has something to do with why certain services won't take our calls."

"Reeally," Lara drawls out, clearly loving this shit.

"Exaggeration," I growl as Bowie grunts something that sounds a lot like "Understatement."

Her answering laugh is something else. A warm, contagious thing, that pulls me along for the ride.

Grinning, I nod toward the cutting board and paring knife. "Grab those for me?"

She reaches for them and our knees brush, just long enough for me to notice how *not* terrible it feels and then mentally slap myself.

We've talked about this. "We" being me and me.

Friends don't notice shit like that.

She sure as hell didn't. Nope, she's just chatting away with Piper as Bowie sets up the Xbox. That easy, gorgeous smile shining so bright it warms the entire room. It's distracting enough that I almost don't mind when Bowie pulls my sister onto his lap and hands her a controller.

Lara

THREE HOURS in and not only am I still the reigning queen of *Call of Duty* but I've totally usurped Ben as champ for *NHL15* too.

"In your face, Boomer," I cheer amidst his excuse-making and protests lodged from where he's standing on the couch.

"If we were playing the new one—"

But I'm waving him off, coming up to my feet as well, then moving to stand on the padded arm so I can get right up into his face. "No, no, no, no, no. The whole purpose of *retro* margarita game night is to play the games from *high school*. Might I suggest a little *Fallout 4*?"

Ben's smile grows. "You're going down."

"Better Chapstick up, buddy. We both know the only one going down is you," I taunt, tequila and wins fueling my bravado.

"Ha! You wish. Assume the position, Elliot, because you're so getting spanked." Ben springs over the coffee table with the remains of our snacks and drinks, clearing it with that same panty-melting athletic grace I've been trying to ignore since we met.

"Pretty sure I didn't invite a date over, so nope. But you—"

A throat clears, and Ben and I both look at where Bowie's watching us with a single raised brow and Piper's head resting wearily against his shoulder. Their controllers are on the table where they've been for a while, now that I think about it.

"Oh sorry!" I squeak. "You want to play something else?"

Bowie chuckles, helping a tipsy Piper up and then holding her hand as they start toward the door. "Much fun as all this *spanking* and *going down* you guys have planned sounds, think this might be our cue to head home."

Instantly, I feel the rush of heat pushing into my cheeks. "When you say it like that—"

"It sounds exactly like when you said it?" Piper grins back at me.

Whoa.

I blink.

Ben blinks.

Bowie pulls Piper against his chest with an indulgent smile and kisses the top of her head. "Time for bed, sweetheart."

I'm like ninety-five percent sure Ben missed the saucy look his little sister just gave his best bud, because if he hadn't... I'm one hundred percent sure Bowie would have been limping out of here.

As it is, I follow them to the door and lock up while Ben gathers glasses and the chip bowl, signaling the fun and games have ended.

I grab a few more empties and follow him into the kitchen where he's rinsing and loading into the dishwasher.

"It doesn't make sense," I say, propping a hip against the counter.

He looks up, mouth hooked in a hint of a smirk. "What?"

"They talk about you like you leave smelly socks and week-old burritos everywhere you go, but from where I'm sitting, you seem pretty neat."

His eyes are back on the dishes, and I'm watching the tips of his ears turn red.

"Used to be... worse."

"Uh-huh." I nod. Then shake my head. "That what happened with the off-ice player business too... or is there maybe another reason you haven't brought anyone home since I moved in here?"

Ben stops moving. He just stops, hands still hovering over the glass he loaded.

And suddenly, I feel like I've overstepped. "Oh my God, I'm sorry. That's none of my business."

He shakes his head, straightening but still not looking at me. "You asking because you want to bring someone back here yourself?"

What? "*Me?*"

"Yeah," he laughs. Sort of.

Turning, he matches my posture from the other side of the dishwasher. "I know you said no relationships. But if you're talking about something... else. Um, of course you can have anyone over you want to."

I force my mouth to close. But then, "Okay. Well, thanks. It's not why I was asking though. I really just didn't want to be the reason *you* weren't living your life the way you like to."

His mouth pulls into a wide grin. "Promise. You're not."

7

_____

Ben

Fine.

    Physically, I respond to Lara Elliot. I'm resigned to that hot fist of attraction tightening every time I see her. Think about her. Yeah.

It's not going away. I thought maybe the closer we got as friends, the less I'd notice the stuff friends aren't supposed to notice. Like how good she smells when she walks by. How her shirt rides up when she gathers her hair into a bun. And how her laugh does something to me I can't explain but know I like too much.

Turns out, the opposite is true.

The closer we get as friends, the harder it gets not to think about certain things. Especially since game night and those awful three seconds when I thought she was asking about bringing a guy home... and this really fucking unpleasant thing happened in my chest.

Like some long-dormant caveman busted free... and decided to liberate his equally thick-skulled buddy downstairs. Because now? Hell.

Every time she tips her head back and laughs, Big Ben takes notice, wanting a better look for himself. A longer look. Closer.

Told myself it doesn't *mean* anything. It's muscle memory, period.

And talking Big Ben down hasn't been a problem, until now.

I peer at the tent in my shorts. The one that's been on the rise since the damn dream I just woke up from. We were back at Belfast Bar. Talking. Laughing. And then it was just the two of us, the place emptying out in a blink. And instead of leaving like normal people, dream me pulled Lara onto my lap. Her breath caught and her eyes startled just a little before going soft, and I could practically feel the air change between us. See echoes of her want from another time and place.

Christ.

And then I blinked again, and my alarm was going off and I was lying in bed thinking about that first night. When we swore it was just going to be the one time and that we'd never, *ever* cross out of the friend zone again.

Such cute kids. So dumb.

Prom— and I'm talking our private after-party, not

that boring-AF dance and dinner —had been a fucking revelation. One night with Lara, hell, one kiss, and it was like my world went from black and white to color.

Kissing my ex— fooling around with her —had felt good, sure. But after having a taste of what it was like to kiss Lara, to touch her... It explained a lot about why waiting had been so easy.

The chemistry between me and my ex had been *meh*, not strong enough for either of us to get carried away.

But with Lara? Damn, I knew it was different the second my mouth met the soft press of hers. I'd swear she did too, with that startled little gasp and deep searching eyes. The way she drifted back within the span of a single breath, lips parting as she pushed to her toes for more, deeper, longer.

As I cupped her face with one hand and slid the other around the small of her back to hold her closer because holy hell, I couldn't get close enough.

As our mouths crashed together, like we'd been waiting for this forever... without even knowing it.

Shit, shit, shit.

I glare down at my dick— the fucker's standing tall, shoulders back, all, *There's plenty more where that came from, buddy.*

Dude, like I don't know.

I've got a hundred memories of the woman sleeping on the other side of this wall. A thousand. Sweet, feisty, patient, furious, and everything in between. Every single one stirs *this* physical response, when mentally?

That's a hard *Hell, no.*

Been there. Done that.

Do not recommend.

Now Big Ben just needs to get with the program. And since, he's particularly bullheaded this morning... I pull out the big guns, flipping through the mental index of shit-you-can't-unsee until I land on the memory of my post-op nut.

Desperate times. Drastic measures.

Blah, blah, blah.

And as he draws back in horror, all *How could I??!* I grumble, "You did this."

Whatever it takes. Because hanging out with Lara again is good. No way am I going to fuck it up. Not when we both know which lines not to cross if we want this friendship to stick. I know I do.

Ben

THESE CHARITY GIGS are part of playing for the Slayers. Bowie and I take them in stride. But tonight, not so much.

No idea what crawled up Bowie's ass, but he's been off all evening.

Yeah, he's pulling it together for what always feels like a thousand handshake photos with the donors at tonight's charity shindig, but every time I lean over to tell him a joke or catch his eye to silently commune over whatever ridiculous thing some douche is saying, the guy gets all twitchy and looks away.

My man is tense.

He's the emotional type. Carries that shit in his shoulders and needs to unload it.

A year ago, we'd go home and shoot the shit, watching sports highlights. I'd nag. Eventually, he'd open up. And miraculously, shoulders unburdened.

Now that he's living with Piper, no idea how the poor guy unwinds.

After a few hours of chatting up donors, dodging the advances of a particularly persistent woman who tried to corner me outside the bathroom, and bringing in bank for a good cause, it's time to clock out. I thank the coordinator for putting everything together and meet Bowie at the side exit.

Not our first rodeo. Going out the front makes it way too easy for some of the hardcore fans to follow us.

Inside his car, I pull out my phone to text Lara we're on our way back.

Big Ben is still trying to butt his head into places he doesn't belong, but he'll get the picture any time now.

"Hey, man, I know it's late, but come get a drink with me?"

It *is* late. But even though my body is dying to get horizontal and my brain is curious to hear how Lara's pitch on this hotel project went, it's been a minute since Bowie and I chilled on our own.

"What you thinking?"

We used to hang out at this club— it was our default place —but after some serious BS with the manager and my sister, it's off the island for good.

He's quiet long enough that I turn to make sure he's okay.

And my man looks... Not quite right. My gut tenses, and I hear the blood rushing past my ears.

Holy shit.

Is he having problems with Piper? No way. They are nauseatingly in love.

Right?

Except now that I think about it, they were going round about Piper wanting to have a party at their place after the Friends and Family Skate at the arena next week. Neither of them seemed pissed, but Piper was pushing, and Bowie was pushing back.

I wouldn't call it fighting, not in the way they usually fight.

But... now my mind is speeding, asking a million questions at once. Like whether there's more going on with them than I know about. And if I'm going to have to break my buddy's face for breaking my little sister's heart... or talk him down from the ledge because she's about to break his.

No. No way.

I'd know. Would have seen something. Anything.

But as soon as the thought crosses my mind, I'm reminded of their bang-up job keeping the truth from me when they first got together.

Gulp.

Bowie clears his throat. "How about that place around the corner we never go to."

I do a double take.

"The Hidden Bridge?" Um. There's a reason we never go there. Not our speed. Too slow. Too quiet. Too moody, maybe?

"Yeah, that's the one." He looks out the driver's-side window like he doesn't want to make eye contact. Or to check traffic, but my gut's picking up an option-A vibe.

Damn.

We don't talk until the car is parked and we're almost at this weird-ass bar that's been haunting the backside of our otherwise cool block. I want to give Bowie the chance to explain what's happening in his own time, but "awkward silence" is my least favorite setting, and apparently he's willing to live there.

I finally crack. "This about the Friends and Family thing?"

Bowie trips on the sidewalk, his head whipping around as he gapes at me.

Bingo.

I take a deep breath and reach for the door to this dark hole in the wall, holding it open as I wave him through.

"Seriously, dude. Get with the program." I've got this. Their relationship is safe in my hands. "Compromise and communication are essential components to being a power couple."

Bowie looks up at me, one brow lifted, all *WTF*. "Power couple?"

"Umm, yeah. As in, your love was enough to make me change my dickish ways, find forgiveness in my heart. Be a bigger man, better friend. Hotter all around."

He shakes his head and drags a hand over his face. "Right."

At the bar, I look around. This place isn't so bad for one drink.

Bowie flags the older guy drying glasses. "Four shots of Jack and a couple of the IPAs you've got on tap."

I blink.

Okay, then. Bowie knocks back one of the shots before the others are even poured and then nods for me to do the same.

So yeah. Whatever he's about to tell me... I'm not going to like it.

～

Lara

SOMETHING'S up with Ben and has been since he came home last night.

Completely bombed.

Arm slung around Bowie's shoulders.

Both men looking suspiciously like they may have been crying.

Bowie sloppily passed him off to me, leaving Ben with a wordless fist-bump before turning down the hall toward the room that used to be his, then backtracking, bumping into the doorframe, and finally making his way out.

Yes, I texted with Piper to make sure he made it the one floor up and got home safely.

This morning, Ben was up before me— typical — but instead of working out, he was just staring out the window— not typical.

I went to work. Came home. And guess who was still staring out the window?

Enough's enough.

"You're being weird." And in case I needed more evidence, Ben makes a face. Waves a dismissive hand through the air, twice. And then makes this sort of *pfft* sound... all within a span of about two seconds.

Totally weird.

After more weird window staring, followed by weird aimless walking around the apartment, he comes back to where I'm working on the couch and drops onto the cushions at the far side, leaving a few inches between his hip and my toes.

I resist the impulse to slide my feet into his lap, digging my toes into the space between the cushions instead. "Boomer?"

Those big blues snap to attention. "What?"

"Everything okay with you?"

God, I hope it's not his job. He's been working so hard to be ready for the team training camp next Monday. He hasn't said anything— at least not to me.

Maybe that's what last night was about.

Maybe he talked to Bowie.

A flurry of emotions pass over his face, none lasting long enough to stick. And then, instead of answering, he asks, "You're coming tomorrow, right?"

"The thing at the arena for family members?" I set my laptop on the coffee table. It's the team putting it on... sooo whatever's bothering him, it's *not* a work thing?

"Yeah."

"I don't know. It was really nice of you to invite me, but—"

"It's for our friends *and* family." He reaches for my foot and pulls it into his lap, that funky mood clearing as the seconds stretch. "You've known me, Bowie, and Piper since high school... So, *friend*. But hell, at this point, you probably count more as family anyway."

I'm not so sure about that. "But—"

My Dad's ringtone plays on my phone, and for a beat, confusion muddles my thoughts. *It's not Sunday.*

"Lara. Hey, you okay?" Ben asks, his eyes shifting between mine, the phone on the coffee table, and my shaking hand as I try to reach for the phone. But I'm sitting weird and it's just out of reach, so Ben hands it to me as I sit up.

"Dad? What's wrong? Are you okay?" I ask, stomach in knots.

"I'm fine, Lara. The job is fine, money's fine, apartment's fine."

Most people probably don't start calls with their family like this. It's a routine we've adopted over the years to reduce the ulcer-breeding anxiety that tended to accompany calls from my dad.

There was only ever one really bad call, but it was the kind that stuck with you.

It came during a sleepover, interrupting a *Wii Sports* marathon. My dad had to pick me up. Right then. So we could pack whatever we could fit in the back of the minivan because the landlord was only giving us an hour to get our stuff. Because he'd already given us two months. And then two weeks. And then another day. But our time was up.

So now we call on a schedule. And anything outside of that schedule is an emergency.

I take a breath, but it's still strained. "Good. That's great. So what's going on?"

Ben's hand is on my back, warm and steady. Grounding.

He probably thinks I'm crazy, except as quickly as the thought surfaces, it's gone. Because I know he won't. He knows about the call. He knows we lived in a car for two weeks. He knows that my relationship with my dad can be a little... intense.

He's just never had a front-row seat before.

"Jimmy Olsen messaged me on Facebook. There's a picture of you and that Boomer kid."

Ben tenses beside me, and I feel my face turning red. Because now I know what this is.

It's the kind of thing only my dad would consider an emergency.

"He's got you thrown over his shoulder and from the way— Lara, there's nothing going on with you two, is there?"

That steady hand at my back becomes a friendly pat, and then Ben heads into the kitchen, leaving me to my mortification.

I know the picture my dad's talking about.

Someone caught us goofing around after a night out. And yeah, there's something about it... the way Ben's hand is on my thigh, how he's grinning back over his shoulder while I'm laughing back over mine... it *looks* like there's more happening than there actually is.

"Dad, 'that Boomer kid' is the same guy you've known and liked since we were in high school. He's the man who opened his apartment to me when I needed a place to stay. We're friends."

"You know I don't care if it's more than that— he's a nice-looking man. And you always had a good time together. So, a little fun. Sure. Nothing wrong with taking care of your physical needs."

There's a clatter in the kitchen, and I desperately try to turn the volume down on my phone, but I'm too out of sorts and just end up putting us on speaker.

"Oh, God."

"We all have them."

"No, Dad. Stop. *Please*."

His chuckle booms through. "All I'm saying is, have your fun. Just don't let some attachment get in the way of your priorities."

"I won't. It's not like that with us, anyway."

"That's my girl."

We wrap up the call with the usual assurances about savings and job security. He tells me he's proud of me, he loves me, and he'll talk to me next Sunday. We end the call, and I just sit there a moment, letting it settle.

Ben reemerges from the kitchen. He sets two waters on the coffee table and reclaims the spot beside me on the couch.

For a minute we don't say anything.

Then, quietly, "You okay?"

"I will be. I mean, the embarrassment's probably going to burn eternal."

"But the call itself."

"It's stupid. I don't freak out about calls from anyone else. I wish I didn't with him." But even after knowing everything is fine, the anxiety is there, sitting heavy in the pit of my stomach.

Ben reaches for me, pulling me onto his lap. His arms are around me, and my head is against his chest.

He runs a hand up and down my arm. Calming. Soothing.

Slowly, that dready sensation inside me unlocks, evaporating until eventually it's gone.

I take a slow breath, knowing I'm going to have to get up but not quite ready to leave the comfort of his hold.

Ben lifts his chin from where it was resting atop my head. "Sooo... I'm like ninety percent sure your dad basically just told you to use me for sex."

"Yeah. He did."

I can feel that smile above me.

"You gotta come to the Friends and Family thing now."

I laugh into his chest, so grateful to have him back in my life, all I can say is, "Okay. But do I *have* to skate?"

Lara

I WASN'T sure about coming today, but now that I'm here, watching all these big, tough hockey players showing off and goofing around on the ice with their loved ones, I am so glad Ben asked me. And while I don't know the team as well as everyone else here, it's a welcoming group.

Even to a non-skater.

Or maybe because of it.

Natalie Vassar helps me tie my skates while her bestie George O'Brien spouts advice meant to keep me off my ass. April Boerboom gives me a hug that literally squeezes the air out of me and then holds my hand for a heart-racing, knee-knocking, slow-motion loop around the rink, *tsk*ing about how her son should have taught me to skate back in high school.

He offered.

I declined. Strongly. A decision I mightily regret right now.

And Ben?

I almost wish he'd abandoned me. It might be easier than all his attentive check-ins.

His questioning thumbs-up from across the ice. His exit from a conversation with another group to give me a tip about balance. His eyes on me so often when I look up to find him, I might do it more than I should.

Even with everything going on today and all the people he's friends with, he doesn't forget about me. It's nice. In a platonic sort of way. Which is all I want despite the ovarian incident taking place at the sight of him skating by with one of his teammate's kids— a *toddler* —hanging from his pinkies.

That little cutie skates about ten times better than me. And over his itty-bitty Slayer's Hockey hat, Ben's flashing me his signature grin, mouthing, *"I'm his favorite."*

It's like this man is made of boyfriend material, and I have no idea how no one can see it but me.

Obviously, I can't have him that way. I *don't* want to. But...

He swoops the little guy off his tiny hockey skates and whispers to him.

Next thing, I'm getting a kiss blown from across the ice from, well, the second-cutest male out here.

Swoon.

"Lara, right?"

I nearly wipe out, turning toward a woman about my age with fiery red hair who introduces herself as Misty Nichols and the player whizzing past her with an X-rated wink as her husband Noel.

She's got a huge smile and this look in her eyes I'm starting to recognize.

"So—" She nudges me with her elbow and then quickly catches me close when I start to slip. "You knew *Boomer* in high school?"

It's like she's asking if I knew Elvis.

"I did. And Grant Bowie was a year ahead of us, and Piper was a few years behind, but yes."

Another woman with similar features but darker hair glides in, introducing herself with a smile. "Stormy Diesel, the nosey one's sister."

I nod, going off balance again, and they both laugh, hooking their arms through mine.

"Thank you," I gasp, trying not to be too obvious about pinning their arms in place. "Nice to meet you both."

Misty bites her lip, searching the crowd. "I can't even imagine him as a kid."

Stormy leans in conspiratorially. "He was the guy hooking up with all the hot teachers, wasn't he?" I open my mouth to tell them no, that Ben was actually as far from promiscuous as a guy could get. But just then, two steel bands clamp across my middle, plucking me from the safety of Misty and Stormy's bracketed arm lock.

"Ben!" I shriek, flying, my skates inches above the ice as he holds me firm against his chest. "Put me down... but *safely*... against the wall."

Preferably by one of the exits so I don't have to skate too far for my escape.

"The *boards*," he says, his voice low and warm, tinged with humor. He's holding me so close his mouth is level with my ear. And, yeah. That fluttery business in my belly I will absolutely be blaming on the way he is effortlessly whisking me around the ice... and not the feel of his breath against the sensitive skin beneath my ear.

When we reach the far end, it's mostly empty. He sets me close to the boards but not close enough. I look at them with longing, and he laughs, taking my hands in his.

"The girls pumping you for information?" he asks, pulling me in and then doing something with his skates that propels him slowly backward.

"You know they were." I watch him move, trying not to give in to the lure of his denim-clad thighs. Failing.

"Tell 'em how you corrupted me?"

I cough, my eyes flashing to his. "Come again?"

"Yeah, pretty sure that was the gist of it." He draws me in, drifts back. "'More, Ben... Again, Ben... Make me co—'"

Laughing, I pull my hand free of his, pushing my fingers across his mouth as his eyes dance with mischief.

"If memory serves," I whisper, ignoring that back-of-the-brain warning that this is territory better left unacknowledged. "It didn't take much arm-twisting. And if anyone was begging—" I glance around, making sure no one is close enough to hear. "It was *you*."

He nips at my fingers, but when I pull my hand away, he catches it again.

"One hundred percent," he concedes with a scorching grin.

And that might have been that, a throwaway reference to times gone by... if our eyes weren't still locked in a hold I couldn't pull away from if I wanted to. And suddenly the memory is there.

His lips at my ear, his perfect body working into me. Deep and deeper. His voice rough, panting... *"Give it to me, Elle. Need to feel you come for me one more time. Please."*

I blink, my breath catching on a sound I definitely don't mean to make.

And when I look back at Ben, that playful smirk is nowhere to be found. The way he's looking at me now—eyes dark, nostrils flaring —I stop breathing altogether.

We draw together.

Drift apart.

Draw together. His eyes move to my mouth.

Come to a stop, mere inches separating us.

Inches that suggest it's not too late to stop what's happening.

Inches that seem to evaporate with my next heartbeat. I don't know if it's me pulling him closer or if it's him pulling me, but the air between us feels different. It's crackling with something hot and electric and as compelling as gravity.

My lips part, and he groans, his hold on my hands tightening—

Abruptly, the music changes. Boomer blinks, the connection gone like it never existed.

He shakes his head and then grins as he drops my hands. "They're playing my song."

My brows lift. "'Gangnam Style'?"

"Don't go anywhere," he says, gliding backward a few feet and then hop-skipping over the ice in the other direction.

Like I could.

He's skating to the beat, pulling one over-the-top dance move after another, clearing a wider and wider space around him.

Until somehow, his maneuvering has opened up center ice... leaving only Bowie and Piper in the middle. Out of nowhere, Boomer drops to one knee and slides like some ballroom dancer across the ice until he stops in front of a smirking Bowie.

What the heck?

And then, I'm coughing out a laugh as Ben reaches into his pocket and pantomimes opening a ring box and holding it up in offering.

What a goof. Such a relief to see him more relaxed than he's been these last couple days. Maybe all he needed was to cut loose on the ice with his friends.

Bowie shakes his head, reaching down to pull his buddy up.

It's all silliness... or is it?

There's something in Ben's face as he stands, an emotion that doesn't quite match the moment.

And in the next second, Bowie pulls him into a hug that tugs at my heart and tightens my throat.

Piper is standing by with a look on her face that says

she may be thinking the same thing. When the two men part, Ben is smiling his brilliant smile as he begins to skate backwards.

His eyes flick to mine, and my heart skips. It all makes sense... because then it's Bowie going to one knee. He holds up a pale blue box.

Oh wow. *Wow.*

A hush falls over the arena. Piper's hands fly to her mouth. And then she's nodding, wiping at teary eyes as she answers with a breathless, "*Yes!*" that carries across the ice.

The crowd goes wild.

Bowie bursts to his feet, and she flings herself into his hold, burying her face in his neck.

He holds her against him, hands fisted in the denim of her jacket, as his shoulders quake once.

My eyes return to Ben. He's got a hand over his chest and he's blinking hard. Those joyful blue eyes find mine and lock. He points to his sister and best friend before mouthing a single word: "*Love.*"

Smiling through tears, I nod.

It's beautiful. It's why he asked me to come tonight. He didn't want me to miss this. And also it's one more reason Ben Boerboom will always take up more room in my heart than I mean to let him.

8

Ben

Bowie, Piper, and I stick around the arena a few minutes to say goodbye to my parents and thank the staff who helped coordinate the big event. The guys in PR look like Christmas came early this year and are still throwing rapid-fire ideas about coordinating team promo with wedding ideas as we wave goodbye and hit the sidewalk.

It's a gorgeous night, too warm for the light coats most of the family were wearing on the ice. So I've got Piper's over my arm since Bowie's are filled with her... and she hasn't stopped kissing all over his face since he stuck that giant-ass ring on her finger.

I risk a backward glance and wince, once again confronted by the reminder of why Bowie was trying so hard to avoid a party after skating. He wanted to be alone with her. So they could celebrate. Privately.

Gah.

Gonna need a solid brain-bleaching after this.

Or just my favorite, most effective distraction.

Last I saw, Lara was being swept along in a tide of WAGs headed to the Five Hole. She was laughing with them, looking like she fit in the same way she always does.

The woman makes friends as easily as breathing, but I want to make sure she's doing good. Having fun. That my mother didn't corner her and try to get her to marry me or something.

Least I can do after pressuring her to come along, right?

So maybe my strides eat up the sidewalk a bit faster than usual. So what. Better than hanging back while Bowie and Piper score a public indecency arrest.

The walk to the bar is quick, and the place is hopping. Not so much the front, which doesn't get that busy on non-game nights. But the back rooms we rented out are packed.

And holy shit, they've even opened upstairs. I clap the hired muscle at the ropes dividing the two areas on his beefy arm and step into the fray.

My heart is hammering as I scan the crowd for Lara. Muscle memory. That's all.

And then I catch her. She's standing over by the bar,

head thrown back laughing. Fuck, the sexy length of her neck makes resisting non-platonic thoughts a challenge. But I rise to that shit. Also, what else is new.

I'm already heading her way when my laser focus expands enough to see who's got her laughing. I grind to a stop, brows crashing down.

Static comes up in my peripheral. "Jesus, man. Gulls takes your place on the team last season, and you have no issue with him. But he spends five minutes talking with Lara, and you look like you're about to take his head off."

"Nah." I want to mean it. But then Trevor fucking Gulbrandsen touches her, and shit starts to short-circuit in my head.

"Whoa, whoa, whoa." Static laughs, sticking his arm out, clothesline-style. "Chill out, man, it was a high five."

I try to unlock my jaw before my molars turn to dust, maybe to tell him I'm fine. But all I can manage is a grunt.

"Yeah, I hear you." He nods beside me but then squints and shakes his head. "But I'm like *ninety-nine percent* sure he's not into your girl there."

"Wrong." I don't buy it. She's fucking gorgeous. Smart. Funny. And when she looks into your eyes— I shake my head, feeling that achy pull in my chest.

Static holds up his free hand up. "Sorry, not *your girl*. I meant to say the girl you know in a biblical sense from back in the day, currently live with, and can't keep your eyes off anytime you're in the same room... but who most definitely *isn't* yours. Cut the kid some slack. For real, he's not into her."

I wasn't saying she isn't mine... even though she isn't. But, "What makes you think he's not into her?"

"You didn't see him over at the arena?"

I saw him with a few people I didn't know, but truth? Between Lara and the impending proposal, most of my bandwidth was taken up. I didn't get around to saying hi. Figured I'd catch up with him when camp starts Monday.

But that was before this bullshit. Because Lara's laughing *again*. And whatever just came out of his mouth makes me want to put my fist in it.

Which isn't me.

It isn't.

I'm a lover, not a fighter.

And Lara?

Not. My. Girl.

I don't even want her to be. But motherfucker, no fucking way can I watch her become one of my teammates' either.

Static says something else, but I'm not listening. I push Piper's jacket into his chest and start walking.

I'm not going to start anything.

Nope. Just going to make a point.

People turn as I cut around them. I nod and keep moving until I'm nearly there. Lara sees me first. Her head tilts, and she gives me a curious look that only gets more confused as I sweep her up into my arms for a hug that pulls her off her feet, and then set her down... leaving my arm around her back in a blatantly possessive hold.

Like a total douche.

But instead of Gulls giving me some contrite look and backing away with his hands up, the guy grins wide and sticks his fist out for a bump. Huh.

My eyes cut back to Static, who's pointing off to the side. But I can't see past this guy I don't recognize walking by.

Except then, instead of walking past, the guy stops beside Gulls, who hands him a beer and slides an arm around his waist... just like mine is around Lara's.

Oh *hell, yes*.

"Boomer, you meet my boyfriend Cam yet?" Gulls asks as I shake his man's hand with a big grin.

"Good to meet you, Cam." So good. Because not only is Trevor in a relationship, the way he's looking at his boyfriend says it's the real deal.

Aww. Love.

It's everywhere today, and I'm kinda digging it.

Catching the bartender's eye, I signal for a round— "Tequila." —and then I snug Lara into my side, because, yeah, I'm not letting her go.

Lara

I CAN'T STOP LAUGHING.

No idea how long we've been at this bar, but there have been shots. Then water. Then more shots.

And instead of winding down, the party only seems to be getting started. Enough people have arrived that the owner brought in another bartender.

We're sitting with Piper and Bowie, who's detailing the strategic planning that went into telling Ben about his intention to propose.

"It was practical," Bowie announces, tipping back his beer with an uncharacteristic grin. "I figured there was a chance greater than zero that if Boomer, here, decided he really didn't like what I was saying... there might be an 'incident,' and at least it would happen in a bar we wouldn't miss if we weren't allowed back."

Ben's nodding, like this makes perfect sense. No denial. Just the tip of his bottle toward his buddy before looking around the table. "Turns out, the Hidden Bridge slays."

Piper climbs out of Bowie's lap and rounds to her brother, ruffling his hair in a way I wish I could get away with. "So, good thing you didn't start flipping tables, huh?"

"What? Me? Nah. Not when Bowie was stand-up enough to ask my permission to marry you."

Bowie rolls his eyes, muttering, "Wasn't actually *asking*."

My beer almost comes out of my nose, but Ben rolls right on.

"Now if you were telling me you got her pregnant..." He makes a face like he doesn't even want to think about it. "Things might've ended differently."

"He's not joking." Piper slips into the space beside me, a knowing smirk on her face. "I'm not even sure Bowie will be safe once we are married."

I don't want to be the one to say it. But, "Probably not."

We dissolve into laughter as Ben slaps the table, announcing he's getting another round. Bowie goes with him, and I watch, hating myself a little for lingering on how good he looks from behind. For thinking that the right girl at the right time—

I cut myself off from a train of thought no good will come from.

Piper watches them as well, then looks down at her ring. She bites her lip before turning to me, eyes glittering like the stone that's throwing light in every direction. "I still can't believe this is happening. That he's mine."

My heart melts and I nod. "He is. Made sure the entire city knew it too."

Her smile grows impossibly wider. "Yeah, he did."

Then, "You probably don't know this, but I've been in love with him since I was a kid. I never thought—"

And now I'm pretty sure my eyes are glittering too. "I remember thinking you were pretty cute with your crush, but I didn't realize how deep it went."

She cocks her head. "I wanted it to go away. For years. I hated that I couldn't get past my feelings. And then... *finally*."

And then finally it's like you can breathe. I understand better than she knows. "You got your happily ever after. I'm so happy for you, Piper."

"Me too. Thank you." She pulls me in for a hug that leaves me feeling emotional and messy. Joyful. Bittersweet. "Now if Ben would grow out of his epic fuck-boy phase, my mother will finally be able to rest."

And that's just the reminder I need, at just the right moment too. "I haven't seen it firsthand, but he said he doesn't date." And then there's all the gossip.

"Understatement."

I laugh. "That bad?"

There's no way.

She leans back with a sigh. "*Worse*. The stories—and they won't even tell me all of them because I'm his sister. But they're *bad*."

I'm skeptical. "They're *stories*, though. Gossip. I've got to think most of that is exaggeration and rumor, right?" No way would I believe everything I've heard about him.

"I mean, the stuff I'm talking about is from his teammates and the WAGs, not those gross bunny sites. There was this couch." She makes a little gaggy face and leans in to whisper, "They had to *burn* it after."

I blink. "After *what*?"

"Ben and the bunnies."

I blink again, but maybe it's my eye twitching. "Like, *plural*? How many bunnies?"

"A herd of them? Don't know. Again... little sister."

I look back at where Ben is standing with his friends, remember this man when we were eighteen. The way he gasped and fisted the earth when I put my mouth on him the first time. How his brows had shot high in astonishment and then gradually pulled low, knitting together as he watched me like I was delivering an agonizing kind of pleasure that needed his utmost attention. Like he was committing every second to memory.

The way he moved heaven and earth to repay the favor again and again.

Ben's an adventurous, creative guy. But needing to *burn* a couch... is intense.

"I know it's got to be kind of weird when the last time you guys hung out, he was *Mr. Commitment*, looking at forever with *Whatshername*."

Celia.

"A little." And then, I ask the question I don't ever let myself think about. "Do you think it's because of her?"

"The she-devil?" Piper taps her lips, eyes squinting. "I mean, she messed him up, bad. No question about that. But if you're asking whether he got over the girl he was planning to marry..."

Why am I holding my breath? It doesn't matter to me, doesn't play into my life plans. But somehow it feels a little like it does.

"... I honestly don't know. The fact that he won't even say her name suggests some baggage, but that's also just kind of a Ben thing. My bet is that he just isn't quite ready to settle down yet, is all. Few more years though? Who knows."

"Maybe."

9

Ben

We're waiting at the bar for our order when Axel Erikson and Wade Grady come up. It's the usual fist-bumps and bro hugs, but tonight it feels like there's more emotion to it. More love. This team couldn't be happier for Bowie.

"Been a minute since the four of us hung, huh?" Axel's talking to us, but already his eyes are searching out his wife Nora, who's deep in conversation with Harlow Grady across the room.

Bowie nods, but I shake my head. "You get a wife and kid, and suddenly you don't write. You don't call."

Cue the groans and muttering, and my grin just gets wider.

Giving crap is kind of the team love language. Which

is all I'm doing. Regular season, I see my boys every day. Just not usually *here*.

The Five Hole's a good bar and its proximity to the arena makes it a regular spot for a lot of the guys after home games. Thing is, the vibe's normally a little mellow for my amped-up postgame energy. Or at least it was.

Testacalypse changed things with me. The whole club scene hasn't appealed the same way it did before my nut tried out a new yoga pose and got all tangled up on itself.

Maybe it's because I found out the now ex-manager from my formerly favorite hang was abusing his position to push my sister to sleep with him. Or maybe the call of the bunnies just isn't as strong.

Whatever. Tonight, the Five Hole suits me perfectly.

I find Lara still talking to my sister. Her eyes blink up, meeting mine. Damn.

That smile. It does something to me. Gives my chest that too-full, top-of-the-roller-coaster feeling, and fuck, a part of me just wants to throw my arms up and give in to gravity... Fall.

But instead, I'm trying to grip the safety bar, resisting the pull because she's not staying.

The guy behind the bar slides a tray of shots and beer to me. I give him a fat tip and thank him again for coming in on his night off. Balancing the tray in one hand, I pass out shots and beers with the other as I make my way back to our table.

"Ladies," I say with a bow. Then to my sister, "Bowie asked me to send you over if you were free."

Piper pops up to smack a kiss on my cheek and snags one of the shots before heading back to the bar.

Lara beams up at me from her seat. "If this hockey thing doesn't pan out, a career in waiting tables is a solid possibility."

"Right?" I set the tray in the center of the table, handing a shot to Lara and then taking one of my own. "I'm charming as fuck, great balance. Tips? I'd slay."

She flashes me a saucy wink and tucks a single into my front jeans pocket. "Thanks, hon. Get yourself something nice."

Jesus, this girl.

We down our shots, and I grab her hand, pulling her to stand. "Let's go, Elliot."

She gives me an arched brow and a smile that hits me a little lower than it should. *Down, boy.*

"Go where?"

I thumb toward the stairwell at the back, pulling her along. "Dancing."

"Yes!"

We weave through the crowd and climb the stairs, her hand in mine so I don't lose her. At the top, the hallway is roped off to the right, blocking a couple doors

I've never been past and to the left... damn, that's a lot of people.

It's loud, the music's thumping in that way where you can feel it through your organs. I love that shit. Always have. Reminds me of getting pumped up for games.

Already finding the beat, Lara gives me one arched brow. "You still got it?"

That taunting look. In another life, I can see myself answering it with a kiss. Ducking my head and meeting the curve of her lips with the press of mine.

But in this one? "*Oh*, I've got it."

We hit the dance floor, moving together with our friends, with the music on our own.

The energy in this place tonight is off the charts, so different from the usual chill vibe. It's contagious, kinetic... building as people join in.

It's fun.

More shots make the rounds. More sweaty bodies surge together.

Add to that, I'm still riding the adrenaline high that's been burning through my veins since Bowie popped the question scoring him official brother-in-law status. And I'm with *her*.

So we dance. We get low and lower.

We bounce high and higher.

We drink. We bust out our best TikTok moves trying

to outdo each other. Until we're breathless from laughing.

She's fucking amazing. Fun.

Sexy.

She's driving me wild. Feeding that part of me that wishes things were different. Wonders what it might have been like now if they were. Remembers those few weeks eight years ago when they were.

I take her in my arms and give in to the eye contact that locks us into place, holding us there as we find a slower beat. Something changes in the way we move.

Because it just feels too good. Too right. And if ever there was a night I could justify giving in in the name of celebration— this is it.

So my arm falls around her waist. It's dangerous, but we're just dancing. That's all.

Her arms fold behind my neck.

Our thighs slot together.

Our hips sync to a heavier beat.

We're just dancing.

I brush a sweat-damp curl from her cheek, tucking it behind her ear and then letting the back of my thumb skim the length of her neck.

We slow. Stop.

Our eyes are locked, searching.

Her fingers sift through the short hair at the back of my head. Mine curve into the side of her—

Bump.

Someone ducks to grab a fallen phone behind her, and Lara blinks, her breath catching. And when her eyes meet mine again, it's with a stunned laugh and brows high.

"Lara." I reach for her, a kind of desperation I can't make sense of rising in my chest.

But she's backing away, hands up. "I umm— kind of forgot what year it was. Don't worry, I'm good. Just— I just need a minute."

～

Lara

WHAT AM I DOING!

I stop at the top of the stairs and peek past the ropes, hoping for a restroom or anywhere I can hide out a minute while I get my head on straight. Pull myself together.

One minute it was all fun and fooling around. Ben and I hanging out like normal. And then the next?

Ugh.

He must think I'm crazy. Maybe I am.

"Come on." Ben's gruff voice is suddenly at my ear. His hand, wide and warm across my back, smoothly propels me past the ropes and toward the closed door at the end of the hallway.

"Wait, maybe we shouldn't." And he can read that

any way he wants. Because of the ropes, or because being alone together right now might not be the best idea.

He opens the door with an easy smile. "But we are."

I step into a cluttered space lit only by the hallway behind us and two glass brick windows that glow with the light from the street beyond but obscure any view. From the looks of the boxes, crates of glassware, and miscellaneous bar and sound equipment in the center, the room is mostly storage.

We definitely shouldn't be here.

The door closes, muting the music we were losing ourselves in and dimming the space even more.

Ben walks past me, catching my hand as he navigates to an open spot near the first window.

Propping a shoulder against the bricks, he stares. "We were dancing. That's all."

Ha. "You know that's not all."

The fact that he called it out says he knows. He just doesn't want to admit it.

I shake my head with a laugh. "The only thing between me and getting pregnant were two layers of denim." And my birth control.

Ben blinks. Opens his mouth. Closes it.

Okay, maybe that was a little much. "That came out wrong."

Nod. "I want to tell you it was no big deal. Explain why it wasn't. I do. But all I can think is, if what you said is true, you aren't wearing panties. And, fuck it." His mouth splits into a wide grin. "My brain pretty much stopped working there."

I blink. Shake my head and, yeah, fuck it. Smiling myself, I relax into the wall, my body mirroring his larger one.

Then, "Wait." My eyes narrow as I do some clothing math. "Does that mean...?"

Hello, sexy dimple.

He leans closer, whispering loudly enough to be heard over the music from the main room. *"Commando."*

I laugh. I can't help it. Just like I can't help—

"Hey, eyes up here, Elliot."

"I'm trying!" I really am.

The rounded shoulder he isn't leaning on lifts in a half-shrug. "Yeah, I get it. The need to verify the status of your lace thong is weighing heavy on me."

"Thong?" Of course that's what he's thinking.

He bites his bottom lip, blatantly staring at the front of my jeans. "Slayers Red? Help a friend out and show me?"

"You are *ridiculous*." But damn it, just knowing he's thinking about my panties has them dampening as heat coils through my center. Or maybe it started with the dancing.

Which is why we're here.

"Boomer—" I cut off when he shakes his head, growling at the ceiling.

"Hate it when you call me that."

What? "Everyone calls you that."

"You didn't used to." His voice is low, teasing. "You stopped after prom. But even before, every now and then, you'd slip and call me Ben. And one night, you admitted that in your mind, it's who I always was."

I swallow as memories of the night he's talking about rush my mind.

The summer wind blowing through the open windows of his room.

His arms and shoulders flexing as he held himself above me.

The feel of him filling me again and again, finding that singular spot so deep inside.

His name on my lips as I gasped. *Ben.*

The breathtaking satisfaction that filled his eyes.

He wanted to hear it again. Wanted to hear it every time. And so I confessed that in my mind, it's who he was. And then I spent the next eight years thinking about the heated way he looked at me after.

I close my eyes, shaking my head to ground myself in the now. Because thinking about looks like that one is as much of a problem as me getting carried away on the dance floor. At the grocery store. While we're waiting for the coffee to brew... basically anywhere our paths have crossed in the last two months.

We have a past, so it makes sense my mind would make a rare foray into it. But lately it's been happening more than it should. Still, it wasn't until tonight I was actually in danger of acting on that old attraction. And that can't happen.

Our friendship means too much to risk over something I don't have room in my life for. That neither of us is looking for.

I clear my throat. "You're right. In my mind, you're Ben. You always will be. But after all the time and distance, it felt kind of presumptuous... And maybe it's just easier to keep things straight that way."

His crabby *hmm* pulls another laugh from me. Pulls me a step closer because it feels so good to be there. "So, you want me to call you Ben?"

"Want a lot of things." His brows bounce as he rolls backward against the wall so both shoulders meet the brick. His head tips back. "Including a peek at your redhot, lacy thong with my number embroidered on the front."

I watch him as he watches the ceiling, the light from the window painting the hard-cut planes of his face in stark relief. His throat bobs, and the solid mass of his chest rises and falls with each breath.

He's gorgeous. And looking at him like this? "Sometimes I forget that things aren't the way they were between us. I get caught up in dancing and laughing and how easily we fall into place together, and I forget about the lines we aren't supposed to cross anymore." I take a breath and let it go slowly. "So I call you Boomer to remind myself that things are different."

That reminder is the only thing keeping me from reaching out and touching him the way I used to. Catching his belt and tugging him closer. Sifting my fingers through his hair.

Don't think about it.

He nods, pushing himself off the wall to cross the room. He toys with a mic stand and straightens a stack of boxes.

"How's that working out for you?" he asks, still facing away so there's no reading his expression, the slant of his smile, or the light in his eyes. Even his voice gives nothing away. "Calling me Boomer keeping you on the straight and narrow?"

He knows it's not. *"Ben."*

He rubs at the back of his neck and turns. "And did saying my name suddenly tempt you to cross all the lines?"

I know what he expects. A simple, straightforward *no way*. But I can't give it to him.

"Honestly, more than I want to admit."

He runs a hand over his face, letting out a slow breath. "Yeah, same here."

10

Ben

Ha! *Her face.*

Guess she thought she'd be the only one dropping truth bombs tonight. And yeah, I kind of surprised myself too. But now that we've cracked open this can of worms, a part of me feels relieved. Because even though she hasn't been back that long compared to how long she was gone, this girl has become the person I want to talk to more than any other. No one gets me the way she does. So yeah, I want to talk to her... even if it's about her.

"So why do you think we keep forgetting how things are *supposed* to be between us?"

She bites her lip. "I don't know. I've been able to maintain friendships with other men after getting physical. Once the lines were drawn, I never even thought about crossing them again. But with you? *All aboard the struggle bus.*"

There's a war happening inside my brain. The stupid, jealous-fuck side is cracking his knuckles at the mention of these other men. While the vain asshole who shares rent up there is preening over the fact that Lara struggles to control herself with me, after the rest of the unworthy guys she's been with don't even register.

Both of those parts of my psyche are dicks, but I haven't found a way to evict either one. Not sure how I live with them, but somehow I manage.

As for Lara... "I'll tell you what my problem is. Those weeks we had... they were fucking hot."

She gives up a quiet laugh and leans into the wall. "So hot."

"Sauna hot."

Her lips twist. "Old-Tumblr hot."

I groan a little at the memory of watching her dirty feed one night and move closer. "Inferno hot."

"Fresh-from-the-volcano hot." Her voice has gone a little breathy, and I'm about ninety percent sure her thighs just shifted together.

Rubbing my hand over my mouth and jaw, I remind myself I've got a point to make, and it's not that I can still read this woman's body like the best kind of dirty book.

"Lara, the way I remember those weeks... they were hotter than the surface of the sun." I'm right in front of her now, close enough that even in the dim lighting I can see her searching my eyes. "But maybe the reason we're remembering it like that is because, at the time, we didn't have anything else to compare it to."

She blinks and looks away. "Because it was our first time."

I shove my hands in my pockets so I don't reach out to touch her. "It was new. All of it."

New and fucking miraculous. It takes everything I have not to think of all the ways I got this woman to come for me... Fine. I'm still thinking about them.

A lot.

Her nod is slow, grudgingly given.

And I get it. Those weeks are a time that I've protected too. They meant something. They meant everything. A part of me doesn't want to take a closer look at them because I like how they fit into my memories.

But if holding so tight to our past is getting in the way of our future as friends, I'm willing to loosen my grip some. "Our lives were changing at lightning speed back then. High school was ending. You were heading to college. I was hoping to play. There was a lot of uncertainty." Around everything except us. Or that's how I felt anyway.

"Emotions were running hot," she adds.

"Exactly. And then, before there was a chance for things to maybe level out some, we got cut off."

"We didn't have the perspective to judge what was happening."

"Yeah, that's what I'm saying." It's reasonable. Makes sense. Shouldn't bother me, but fuck if it doesn't.

"We were"— Lara's head cocks to one side, her lips curving in a way that Big Ben digs a lot — "*inexperienced.*"

I nod, trying hard not to think about that first time. The feel of her body giving way. Taking me in. Tight and snug around me.

Shit.

"Right."

She bites her lip, eyes tracking over me. "But not anymore."

"Umm." That instinct I've learned to live by on the ice is tapping its stick.

And now she's nodding, taking a step in my direction. "We'd have the perspective to judge now."

Big Ben stands a little straighter, but my slow nod hangs a Uey and becomes a shake. "I mean, *theoretically.*"

"Mmm."

What the fuck does that soft hum mean, and why am I remembering the time I heard it when her lips were wrapped around my dick?

Okay, this is not what I was planning back here.

"Lara." I lift my hands to signal we should slow

down here, but then she does the one thing I don't have a chance in hell of resisting.

She tucks her fingers around the bottom of her shirt and lifts it the barest inch. Just enough for me to see a ribbon of smooth pale skin. Her thumb hooks into the top of her jeans and my heart stops.

"So, you want to see my panties?"

Fuck. Big Ben nods, throwing his shoulders back, all "Hold my beer," but I've got to think this through.

"I can't lie to you. I want to see them so fucking bad it's killing me to keep my feet planted where they are and not drop to my knees and peel those jeans down your perfect fucking hips right this second."

Her brow lifts, and my body reads it like one of those guys on the tarmac waving a pilot in. I can fucking see it in my mind, each bit of skin being revealed an inch at a time. The silk of some scantily cut lingerie, smooth and tight, damp between her legs—

"Ben." She's laughing, and I snap out of it, patting the air between us, all settle, settle.

But it's more for me than for her.

There's no way we're actually considering this.

I mean, yeah, my thoughts were buried securely in her panties a few minutes ago, but my head goes to a lot of places it doesn't belong. Especially around her. And then when she didn't put the ix-nay on my irty-day musings the way I expected her to... Big Ben started reaching for the wheel.

I'm tempted to swat his big ass away. This is Lara.

But instead of backing off, I take a step closer, because—

This. Is. Lara.

"I don't want to fuck this up. What I was saying, I didn't mean it as a suggestion. I wasn't trying to actually get into your pretty... *pink* panties?" I guess, because, damn, I really want to know. "So much as trying to give us a chance to think more rationally about what might have been fueling some unrealistic memories."

A single finger taps at the denim no longer making a downward descent. *Tap, tap, tap.*

She's giving me her speculative stare. The one where she's working out risk and reward.

I don't know what it is about that look, but from as far back as I can remember, it's been my kryptonite. Her big brain fascinates me, and any time I get to see it at work, I can barely look away.

Then— "I get where you're coming from. Verbal acknowledgement is a good start. But... since it's not like we'd be crossing some line we've never crossed before... wouldn't it be more effective to just give in? See first-hand the experience isn't quite everything we remembered?"

Here's the thing. I know I'm a reasonably smart guy. Top scores in advanced math aside, I wouldn't have gotten where I am in my career if I wasn't. But I can also be rash and impulsive, so a lot of my great ideas need a warning label slapped on them.

But Lara's not rash. She's not impulsive. And her ideas slay.

Which means, if *I* like her idea... and *she* likes her idea... it must be a pretty solid idea.

Either that or Big Ben has stealthily slipped into the driver's seat without me realizing I've handed over the keys.

Lara must not dig the hesitation, because her stance shifts, and she chuckles darkly. "I mean, think what an utter relief it will be once we've done it and it's... *bad*."

I blink, switches in my brain flipping before I fully register the bullshit she just dropped. On purpose. Because she one hundred percent has my number.

"Fuck that, Lara." And then I'm all intent and forward motion, brushing her hands away as I back her up.

Her eyes flare as she lets out a sexy gasp, lips parted on a smile that says she knew exactly what she was doing.

I cage her in with one arm braced above her head and the fingers of my free hand tucking against the button on her jeans. "It's not going to be bad." It could never be bad between us.

"No?"

She's winding me up, playing like she doesn't know. I see her coming a mile away, but fuck if I don't let her anyway. Having her intentions wound up with my reactions feels amazing. It's different with her. So different.

"I'm going to get you off, Lara. And it's going to be really fucking good. It's going to be better than any guy you've had."

"But?" she prompts, hands rushing over my chest and abs.

"But it's just going to be sex. Nothing revelatory. Nothing we can't function around or step past as friends."

"That's what I want."

"I've done this enough—" Enough women, enough ways, enough times when I was searching for that feeling I'd had with her and never finding anything close. "To be able to say with absolute certainty, sex can be fucking amazing... and still just be sex."

Even as I say it, I wonder if it's possible with her. If I'm lying to us both because I want any version of what she's offering too much to resist.

Before I can think too far about it, she says, "Prove it."

Her chin is turned up in a taunt, her eyes burning, lips hooked in a sexy, smile that's just begging me to—

My mouth meets hers a fraction of a second before her shoulders meet the wall. It's a savage, desperate clash of tongues, lips, and teeth. Devouring kisses, hungry hands roaming, grasping at clothing to tug each other closer.

Jesus, she tastes sweet. Like tequila, pure need, and the girl I thought I'd never have to live without.

And yeah, maybe I ought to be concerned that our first kiss is doing things to me an entire night with anyone else in the last eight years couldn't.

But it's just the anticipation. The buildup. Christ, that soft little moan.

My fingers are in her hair, fisting it tight to hold her in place as I take her mouth.

Hers are making quick work of my belt and fly.

I've been horny before, I've been wound up to get in and get off, but this?

Maybe I made a mistake.

Maybe I misjudged. Because this kiss alone?

Maybe I should stop.

I kiss her harder, and she opens to me, clutching at my hair, my shoulders, and my shirt.

Licking into her mouth, I stroke her tongue. Take her breath in and give mine back.

I want to savor this, but there's a short circuit happening in my head that's demanding everything at once. I need the shape of her, the taste of her, the sound of her coming for me. I need to see the rise and fall of her chest, the goosebumps on her belly, and the look in her eyes when I get her close, when I keep her there, when I draw it out because I know it'll make it better for her and because I can't stand the idea of it ending.

I want— fuck, I want more than what this is. But I'm

too far gone to stop over something as trivial as my sanity.

We get this one time.

She's going to have a few mind-blowing orgasms to look back on... They will be a million times better than anything those other fuckers gave her, but they won't be tangled up with all the emotion and newness that got into the mix the first time around.

So I kiss her again, pouring myself into the act of teasing her mouth like the Stanley Cup depends on it.

11

_____

Ben

I lick and nip and soothe, and then I thrust deep, giving her my tongue as she moans around it.

Her hips move against mine, the restless shifting finding a rhythm that has Big Ben about to blow his mind.

It's so fucking good but not enough. Not even close.

"Oh God," she gasps when my mouth trails lower, sampling that sweet spot behind her ear that always drove her crazy.

"Still like this?" I know she does. Can tell by the way her shoulders are bracing against the wall as she tips her head to give me better access.

"Yes, yes. I like it."

Smiling against the warmth of her skin, I ease lower,

to the hollow of her neck as I lift her shirt up, up, and up some more until she has to release her hold on me for it to come off.

Her bra is satiny smooth like her skin, maybe a shade darker. I can't tell in the low light. Just that it's sexy as fuck and even more so when I span my hands over the dip of her waist, up the rise of her ribs, and then press those silk-wrapped mounds to my mouth.

"Fuck, Lara, you have the prettiest tits."

Her answering laugh is soft, breathless. "You may have mentioned that once before."

Yeah, but not because it's some line I whip out as part of my hookup repertoire. It's true.

"So hot." I inch down the cup and brush the tips with my thumbs before catching the right one in a pinch at the same time I give the left my teeth.

And that cry from Lara as her fingers tighten in my hair to hold me closer tells me she likes it almost as much as I do. I open around her, taking as much of her soft breast into my mouth as I can and swirl my tongue over that captured flesh before giving it a deep, slow suck.

Lara

WE'RE IN A BAR.

Rationally, I know this is risky. Something I'd never consider with anyone else, but with Ben? He's always made me feel safe. I don't care about the risks. All I care about is—

Oh my God, this man's mouth!

That cocky laugh.

My knees buckle as a desperate sound slips past my lips, but Ben's hands move to my thighs to support me.

And the sounds he's making, like it's my mouth on him— so hot.

He licks his way to my other breast and covers it the same as before, this time sucking harder, each pull breaking me down, making me gasp and beg as sensation winds a searing path from my nipple to my pussy, cinching tight and tighter. Building the sweet ache inside me.

That smirk against my skin. "Something I can do for you, Elle?"

The words are all innocence, but what he's doing with his tongue is anything but.

"Ben," I gasp.

"What do you need?" he growls against my tight flesh, gifting me with another intimate sensation.

"More. Need you."

Tucking his fingers into my jeans, he flicks the button open. "Time to show me those panties, yeah?"

"Yes." I have just enough brain cells left to go for his belt at the same time, but he brushes my hand away.

"Not yet."

"What?" But beyond that buckle is the good stuff. That buckle is the gateway to Shangri-la.

He pulls back and laughs once. "Don't worry, Elliot. I've got you."

Then he pops up to press a hard kiss to my mouth... before *dropping to his knees.*

My eyes flare, and my breath sucks in with the understanding of what this man intends.

He can't. Not here. Can we? "But— But—"

This is already crazy. But I figure if we skip over some of the sexy times fun— like Ben on his knees doing something I remember he is very, *very* good at — we'll be done faster. And for the purposes of tonight's exercise and the whole not-getting-arrested thing, faster is better.

But then, his face rubs back and forth against the skin between my navel and panties. He tips his head and, blond brow arched, asks, "Want me to stop?"

Cheeks burning with the realization that risk or not, no. No, I do not want him to stop. I frantically shake my head.

Ben starts to lower his gaze, and my body reacts with some kind of Pavlovian response to the proximity of this man's mouth to my pussy. He hooks his fingers in the denim at my hips and inches them lower before pulling away to meet my eyes again.

"You sure?" he asks, pure mischief in his eyes.

This is the Ben I remember, the Ben I loved. And even if that's not who he is most of the time these days, seeing him again is a gift.

I knock his hands from where they aren't making progress nearly fast enough, pushing my jeans down myself. The motion bows me forward, and Ben being Ben doesn't miss the chance to lick between my breasts.

Wow.

I slip my foot from my flat and then out of my jeans leg too. It's a move I perfected in those too few weeks we had together the first time around. One I haven't had the opportunity to use since.

Humming his approval, he takes my hips in his hands and holds me against the wall, eyes focused on the smooth satin of my bikini-cut panties... which are, sadly, more function over form.

"Not quite what you envisioned with the Slayers-red lace thong with your number embroidered on the front."

He swallows, then meets me with an earnest look. "Better."

And before I can argue, he leans forward, opening his mouth over my satin-covered mound.

His mouth is hot, his breath teasing through the fabric in a way that makes me gasp even before he licks the sodden panel between my legs.

He groans, his grip firming on my hips in a hold that feels possessive and as sexy as the lick itself.

"Christ, Lara, I can taste you through your panties. You been getting wet for me all night?"

"Yes."

No sense denying it.

"I gotta see. Gotta feel for myself." His fingers flex at my hip then release enough to skim down the outside of my bare leg, trailing his fingertips over the back of my knee, my calf, and then through the sensitive hollow behind my ankle.

Because he remembers.

Like he remembers that single finger tap, and I remember it's the signal to slip my leg over his arm and then onto his shoulder.

"Just like that, Lara," he praises, guiding my hips forward before hooking a finger to pull my panties to the side, exposing me to his stare, his breath, the flick of his tongue.

"Ben!"

"Dreamed of having you like this again." He shakes his head. "Seeing your pretty pussy glistening for me. Begging me to have a taste."

The noise I make would embarrass me with anyone else, but with Ben, it just feels honest.

"That what you want?" He knows it is, but he's going to make me say it. Own it. "Tell me."

I'm trembling now, his dirty talk making me clench with need. "Please. Taste me."

He brings his thumb to my swollen folds, brushing

them open with an impossibly light touch for such rough hands. His breath reaches my most sensitive spot, and a heartbeat later, his tongue dabs at my clit. He hums his approval.

My fingers knot in his hair, and he groans again like it's what he's been waiting for. And maybe it is because the second I do it, he sinks in, kissing my pussy like he's making love to it.

He runs his tongue over and through me, circling and teasing with the flat before firming it into a point he drags back to my opening where he presses in, lapping and thrusting and swirling around my inner walls.

"Taste so fucking sweet. Can't get enough."

Me either. But— "Ben, please. I want you."

Just once. One more time in my life, I want to feel this man inside me. I want him to hold me up and give me his body while his heart beats against mine.

It's not what we talked about. But the damage is already done. The plan foiled.

Being with him is even better than it was the first time.

"You want me to fuck you, Lara?" He growls against me, and my leg starts to shake.

"Yes," I gasp, clenching in anticipation.

And then it's his finger teasing through my wetness. "I'm gonna. But not until you come on my tongue."

He pierces me again and again, pausing to tell me how sweet I am, how hot I make him, how he needs it.

Needs me to give it to him. And when he returns to my clit, drawing it between his lips to suck, and then suck harder—

"Ben!" I cry, coming apart as he relentlessly pushes me further, carrying me through wave after wave of release until the last bit of pleasure has been wrung free.

Ben turns his head to kiss my inner thigh and then surges to his feet in front of me.

"Inside me," I pant, and he nods, the urgency between us at a fever peak.

He tears open the square wrapper he must have pulled from his wallet at some point and rolls it on in a blur I can probably attribute to all those maybe true, maybe exaggerated rumors. I send up a silent thanks to the scores of women who have come before, because the man is proficient and doesn't make me wait.

And then my arms are around his neck and he's taking me by the hips, lifting me so we align in the place I need him to be.

"Tell me," he grits out, his length sliding back and forth through my sensitized folds before notching himself at my opening.

I'm shaking, my body on fire. I don't know how it's even possible to be this desperate when I've just come harder than I have in the last eight years. But I need him. "Please."

And this man, who has never in my life let me down, doesn't now. Before I can even draw a breath, he's pushing inside. And then I forget breathing altogether because nothing has ever felt this good in my life and every single part of me is focused on the give of my body as Ben stretches me to take him.

He knows he's big and goes slow as he works each steely inch inside, withdrawing and then driving in that much deeper, giving my body the chance to adjust before giving me more. And that wicked, slow advance when I'm this wet, this sensitive, has me trembling beneath his pleasurable assault.

Ben is silent, his grip on my hips tightening in a way that works as well as his dirty talk when he was on his knees.

He sinks deep and deeper, straining my inner walls with the most decadently intense pressure until there isn't any more room at all.

My muscles spasm around him, gripping and grasping as I lift my eyes to meet his.

And the instant our eyes connect, I feel it through every part of me. My heart clenches, my throat goes tight, and my body gives up another bit of space to take just that much more of him.

"Ben," I whisper, my voice unsteady.

"I got you," he murmurs into that scant space between us, giving me longer strokes, harder contact, deep, full-length thrusts that steal my breath and make me cling to his shoulders.

"Want to feel you come." I gasp at his ear. "Want *you* to lose control for me."

His head lifts and he presses his brow to mine. "Want me to fuck you into this wall, Lara?"

I nod, opening my mouth to lick at his in a tease I remember used to work for him. That answering groan says it still does.

And then he's pistoning inside me, driving full-length again and again, faster and faster. Telling me how fucking good I feel, how he loves my body, how he can't get enough. Each word taking me closer, ramping the tension higher, until *I'm there*.

I cry out, spilling a string of unintelligible sounds as pleasure seizes me.

"OhmygodBenyoufeelsogoodsogoodsogood…"

"Fuck, you're perfect," he groans a breath before his mouth slams down on mine, and he goes tense around me… gets impossibly harder… everywhere. And then, with a roar, he comes, rocking our bodies together through his release until we're both still.

Breathless.

Sweaty.

Smiling into each other's eyes, because even if it was only once… it was perfect.

12

Ben

Standing with my hand over the knob of my bedroom door, I roll out my shoulders and tell myself *again*, it's not going to be weird.

So what if I woke up to the memory of her taste on my tongue and my dick so hard it took thirty minutes in an ice-cold shower to talk him down.

Talk. That's all.

Bad as he wanted it, no way was I going to jerk off to thoughts of her after expelling the demons as thoroughly as we did last night. The whole point of fucking each other senseless was—

Okay, the point was to prove that our memories had been exaggerated. And while I don't want to say it to her face, that one's going down in the books as an epic fail.

At least for me.

Being with Lara—

I rub at the ache in my chest that's been there since she moved in but grew like it had been rolling around in gamma rays last night.

I should have known that sex between us, could *never* just be sex.

So why was I trying to convince us both it could?

I glare down at my junk to where Big Ben is conspicuously looking away. But deep down I know he's only part of the problem. Not even the majority of it. And I don't even want to think about the organ truly responsible for this shitshow.

Time to sac up.

I venture into the hall, listening for any hints as to where she is. Probably sleeping. But as I pass her room, the door is half open and her bed is already made.

But then I catch the quiet click of her keyboard and follow it to the living room where she's sitting on the couch, working on her laptop.

She's got a pair of creamy lounge pants on and a loose top in the same stretchy fabric with a wide neck that's nearly slipped off her shoulder. Her hair is up in one of those sexy bun things women call "messy," and from the dozen feet away that I'm standing, I can see a hint of pink along the stretch of her neck where my face was buried last night.

I gulp. She's still wearing me on her skin.

Not something I'd normally get off on, but this morning... well, yeah.

I clear my throat like an ass, and then jut my chin at her like an even bigger one. Fuck. Finally, I choke out a hoarse, "Morning, Elliot."

Her mouth pulls to the side as she watches me. "I made coffee."

And I should definitely have some. Snap out of the tentative, anxious bullshit state I woke up in.

After what's undoubtedly an awkward pause, I clod into the kitchen and pour myself a mug.

Downing half the scalding brew in one gulp, I kiss my tastebuds goodbye. Desperate times, desperate measures.

I need to figure this out.

I'm *not* a tentative guy. I'm fucking reactionary. An act-before-I-think machine who's made a career of running on instinct. But with Lara, the stakes are so high, I'm second-guessing everything. And it sucks.

PS: Where was this evaluative skill set when I was in high school English class?

Leaning back against the sink, I side-eye the living room, telling myself I'm not actually hiding from the woman casually parked on my couch, just out of sight.

What's my problem?

She's being totally normal. From the minute we left that storage room last night. Hell, before we were even out the door.

She gave me a conspiratorial smile while hashing out who'd leave first, where we'd reconvene after a quick cleanup in our respective restrooms, and how long we needed to stay before taking off. Her brain was firing on all cylinders, while mine was locked around the sounds she'd made when I pushed inside her, holding tight to how her lips parted when she came on my tongue and tucking away the feel of her arms around my neck like she never wanted to let go.

I nod, take another swallow.

She's being totally, perfectly, follow-the-plan normal.

Business as usual. Literally.

Which means... maybe last night worked for her after all? I ought to be taking a victory lap and high-fiving her, but my heart wouldn't be in it.

Because how can she be normal, when I'm like... *this*.

The sound of movement from the other room reaches me a second before she steps into the kitchen and comes up beside me to rinse her mug. "So, training camp tomorrow?"

More normal.

I can be normal too. "Yep." I take a breath, ready to elaborate when it hits me—

Coconut. Oh hell. It's in the air around her.

That same sexy scent I was practically huffing last night when I had her wrapped around me, caught in my hold as her sweet body gripped and grasped at me through each thrust.

"Great," she sighs, starting to turn away.

Fuck! "Sorry, Lara, wait. My mind was somewhere else." *Deep, deep in your body, but I'm keeping that to myself.*

Those soft brown eyes turn back to me, and I go on. "Camp starts tomorrow. Some of the guys won't do the full week. But since I was out for playoffs and anything we do off-season has to be separate from management, I want as much ice time with the coaches as I can get."

She leans into the sink beside me, settling in. "So you can catch up?"

I huff a laugh. "So I can show them I'm already caught up. Remind them they don't want to play without me."

Her brows lift and she nods in understanding. "You feel good about it?"

"Yeah, as good as I can without a crystal ball." We talk about what it was like being out last season. How I thought this career I've sacrificed so much for might be over. How it fucking terrified me. I tell her things I haven't told anyone.

And she gets it.

She understands.

And then we talk about training camp and what it's looked like over the years. What I've done this summer to make sure I can hold onto my spot come fall. There's something really nice about sharing my plans like this.

It's the kind of thing a guy could get used to if he wasn't careful.

"Anyway, glad you brought it up. I'll be gone a lot this week with long days and late nights. Might not see you much, and"— *Jesus, just spit it out* —"I don't want you to think it has anything to do with last night."

"Ooh. Okay, sure." She smiles. "Thanks, Ben."

Fuck, I shouldn't have told her to call me that. Begged her, more like.

Her eyes drop to where her hands have come together in a loose hold. "Um, about that. I know we were kind of hoping last night would resolve the tension and all that." She takes a deep breath, and I stop breathing altogether. "And I want you to know, it's totally fine and won't affect anything. I mean, we're good. We're fine. Totally."

"Totally," I say back, feeling anything but, even though I'm pretty sure this uncharacteristic rambly business is her way of letting me know she can tell I'm in worse shape than before I got to sink inside her... but she won't hold it against me.

"Full disclosure?" Those gorgeous brown eyes come up, meeting mine in an apologetic wince. "It didn't work."

∾

Lara

I DON'T KNOW what reaction I was expecting exactly. Maybe something along the lines of somber acceptance, a pained step back, "Sucks to be you!"— Okay, not that last, or really any of the scenarios that have been running through my mind on repeat as I obsessively debated whether to come clean or not.

Ben isn't callous.

He wouldn't make light.

He wouldn't laugh.

Oh. Well.

Okay, apparently, he *would* laugh. But not *at* me.

Head tipped back, this almost relieved sound bursts free. And then he reaches out and pulls me into the hard-packed perfection of his chest, holding me tightly in a way that's somehow both reassuring to my mind and confusing to my heart.

"Ben?" I whisper, trying not to bury my nose in his chest.

He smells so good.

"I've been dying here, Lara. Not sure how to own up to it. Feeling guilty as fuck and more stupid than that for ever thinking— *whatever*." Big hands wrap around my shoulders, and he pushes me back just far enough to meet my eyes. "That plan was an epic fucking fail."

Relief gusts out of me *à la*, "Yes! Oh my God, Ben, I have no idea what we were thinking."

He's nodding, blond brows pushed high. "Right?!"

"And worse, I can't even make myself regret it."

"Exactly! I mean, it's really, *really* hard to regret something that good." He pulls me in for another smothering-but-what-a-way-to-go hug I don't even have time to sink into before he's setting me back again. "Now, if you were upset, I'd hate myself. True story. But since you're not, and you don't think it was a mistake—"

"Oh, don't get me wrong." My hand goes to my forehead. "I *know* it was a mistake. Just one I can't bring myself to feel too bad about, since neither of us got hurt. I mean, what's the harm if it only happens once and we don't let it change anything?"

Ben nods. Keeps on nodding. His eyes still locked with mine. And then he's not nodding at all. He's just looking into my eyes, his hands wrapped around my shoulders, thumbs brushing soft circles as I fist the side of his shirt.

When did I grab his shirt?

"Lara," he says, his voice losing that ramped-up energy of the moment before. "What if—"

He looks away, letting out another slow breath I don't quite know how to read.

He lets me go, bracing his hands on the counter. I step into the spot beside him and wait.

Eyes on the floor between us, he chews on his cheek. "You really don't think it's going to change anything, Elliot?"

I swallow, understanding a bit more about the power of the name you choose in any given moment. "Of course it changes *some* things. But not the way we've become friends again. Not the big stuff, the important stuff. Not if we don't let it." I take a breath. "So maybe it'll be a little weird for a while. So what. If we own it, if we laugh it off, we'll be fine."

Reaching out, he catches my hand in the loose hold of his. "Be weird together instead of weird alone. Pretending it's not."

"Yeah. Exactly."

He hums, checking out the ceiling as his smile reemerges. "Soooo, weird like admitting I'm having trouble pretending I don't notice you're still wearing my beard burn."

I laugh, feeling better to be on the same page with this man. Then letting his hand go, I reach up and give his jaw a light brush with my nails. "More stubble scrape than beard burn. And weird like it took me more than a minute this morning to remind myself that what happened last night is a line we can't cross again. And I'm probably going to have remind myself a few more times."

He turns his cheek into my hand, his body shifting too. "Weird like standing here with you, touching like this feels good, but I'm not sure if it's cool or just the first step on a slippery slope neither of us want to be caught on."

I nod, running my nails over the thick blond scruff, maybe liking it as much as he does. "I like it too. Honestly, trying to remember to keep a physical space between us since I moved in has been tough. Being close like this feels more natural than forcing ourselves to stay apart."

"Yeah?"

He pulls me in even closer for another heart-melting hug I don't know how I managed to live without for so many years. "I like being close to you. Always have."

Head pressed to his chest, I smile. "Me, too."

"Friends totally hug."

"They do. Just not naked."

He huffs into my hair. "So we're good?"

I nod. "We're good."

"And we're going to face the *weird* head-on?"

This guy. "Yes. Totally take its power away."

"Awesome." He pulls back, giving me a sorry, not sorry shrug. "This stretchy business you've got on is hot as fuck, and Big Ben's gonna need a minute after last night to get back in line."

I grin up at him. "Oh my God, 'Big Ben' is going to need a minute?"

"Yes." He adjusts his jeans. "He might need two. He likes your laugh a hell of a lot too."

He walks past me, and I turn, catching him before he leaves.

Should I?

This is Ben. One hundred percent I should.

Smile stretching, I lean in. "If it makes you feel any better, Li'l Elliot might need a minute too."

His eyes blatantly drop to the land where Li'l Elliot reigns. Biting his lip, he stares a beat, while I stand, brow raised. When his eyes bounce back to mine, his smile is equal parts naughty and satisfied... and Li'l Elliot definitely notices.

Down, girl.

13

Preseason

Ben

I ought to be relieved with how easily things fell back into place with Lara.

I *am* relieved.

We've been good since our little kitchen summit last week. Better than.

Not one naked hugging violation on record.

I mean, maybe there was a moment that first morning when I thought about what life might be like between us if we wanted more than just that night. I might even have indulged in a little fantasy about a lifetime of morning kitchen time together. Pouring her coffee. Pulling her into my arms. Knowing this was it.

But that was a temporary lapse in judgment. Fleeting and nearly forgotten.

There's one thing between us that works really fucking well. Friendship. The kind with fully clothed hugs, texting random shit, and talking at all hours.

That's all I'm interested in. It's all she's interested in. That's how we stay friends this time around, no matter where her plans take her.

Thing is, while my heart, my brain, and even Big Ben — all the vital organs —know a *relationship* with Lara is off the table, I haven't quite been able to convince them that more of that breath-stealing, mind-blowing, delectably slippery slope we found ourselves on in that storage room above the bar... isn't a place we want to return to.

In fact, pretty much any time I'm not on the ice, busting ass to show my coaches and management that my rogue nut didn't take me out for good... I'm busting ass to get my mind off the spectacularly good sex Lara and I won't be having again. I shouldn't keep thinking about it, but I am.

I'll get over it. Past it. Whatever. I've done it before... Just not while she was living with me.

Not while we're still sharing dinners and kicking back in front of a game or show. Not when she's close enough to reach for an apple at the same time I do, and when our fingers accidentally brush and then our eyes meet... all I can do is search them for any sign of the way she looked at me when I was inside her.

Wondering if she still feels the connection—

Fuck! The connection that whole night was supposed to eradicate but didn't.

I'll get over it. I will. Because we're friends.

Regular Season

Lara

WE'RE FRIENDS.

Really, really good friends who aren't letting one silly night of misguided intentions and libidos-gone-wild screw it up.

That's what I'm reminding myself as my rideshare pulls up to our building instead of taking me out for drinks with a few coworkers after a grind of a week that isn't even over yet.

It's what I've been reminding myself every night for the better part of two weeks, while trying to ignore the mental replay of what happened above the bar. But it's on loop. In slow motion. With a black-and-white filter and one of those crazy sexy sound clips from the TikTok you accidentally find yourself watching thirty-six times in a row.

It's what I was reminding myself when I broke down and made an online purchase I am hoping will alleviate the growing ache threatening a friendship that has become the most important thing in my life. Because Li'l Elliot has been dreaming of more.

More of Ben's kisses.

More of his firm hold.

More of him, working my body to peak after peak of pleasure, and then doing it all again.

More of that heart-and-soul connection I've only ever felt with him. And okay, maybe that last bit wasn't Li'l Elliot... but since she seems to be the source of most of my issues, I'm pinning the fantasies about things my life doesn't have room for on her too.

The hardest part? It's not just me. I know Ben feels it too— maybe not exactly the way I do. Not as deeply or urgently. Not as emotionally, maybe. Probably.

But it's there when we talk late after one of his games, laughing about some stunt Rux Meyers or one of the other guys pulled in the locker room. It's there when our eyes catch in a way that isn't quite friendship alone, holding until Ben's smile slants to one side and he shakes his head before covering his mouth to sound like a robot, saying, "Danger... danger," and I give up a wry, quiet chuckle, adding a faraway-sounding, "Eject... eject."

At least we can laugh at it. Which is about a million times better than if we couldn't.

And while the residual attraction hasn't quite resolved, it thankfully hasn't gotten in the way yet either. And I'm not going to let it. So I'm taking matters into my own hands, *so to speak.*

The car pulls up to drop me off, and I hastily thank the driver before dashing inside for the mailroom.

I can't believe I bought this. A year ago, this purchase would have been a hard no. Frivolous spending. Unnecessary.

Now?

Critical.

The mailroom is tucked around the back side of the building and only monitored by the attendant during regular business hours most weekdays but on Wednesday until six thirty p.m.

The timing is perfect because Ben's got some PR thing with the team after practice tonight.

Or I thought he did.

When I skid into the mailroom, there's a tall glass of water drumming his fingers over the counter. Ben.

He turns, does a double take, and blanches. "Elliot," he says slowly. "Thought you were out with work friends."

I smile, trying to swallow past my heart... which is securely lodged in my throat, hammering away. "Change of plans. What about you? Weren't you—" Now that I think about it, he didn't actually specify what he was doing. Which is weird in itself.

153

"Cancelled." I'd swear the tips of his ears turn red.

We stare at each other as the attendant returns with a stack of parcels. "All together, okay?"

I very, very much want to say no, but that would only draw more attention to something I very, very much don't want to draw attention to at all. "Sure."

"Yeah, great. I'll take them." Ben reaches for the stack, and my eye starts to twitch.

"Umm, how about I take my stuff out of there. You don't need to carry all of it."

Ben looks down. Then back at me. "Pretty sure I can handle it."

We head to the elevator and stand at opposite sides. Silently.

It's totally weird. But whatever his weird is about... I. Don't. Care.

Just give me my package and leave me on my own.

The doors open and we walk out. Me eyeballing the stack, doing some package math, estimating sizes, weights... and then plotting how to get my hands on the package third from the bottom. I unlock the door, blocking it with my body while Ben crooks a brow.

"You want me to pay a toll or something?"

Actually, yes. I really, really do.

Bad Li'l Elliot!

I force a laugh, grab my package, and sprint for my room. "Sorry! Drank too much coffee... tired... later!"

My door closes out the sound of Ben calling after me.

Not now, Mr. Boerboom.

Hands shaking, I rip into the tape, tearing open the cardboard.

Please let this thing come with a partial charge. It's waterproof. We'll have a shower. Take the edge off, clear the demons, and—

"What?" I was so sure this was my order, it takes a minute for my mind to catch up and register just what I'm looking at.

Three hard knocks sound at my door. "Lara, I think you took mine by mistake."

My eyes narrow, and I stalk to the door.

Swinging it open, I hold out his delivery— two sets of men's reusable rubber gloves for household cleaning. *"Sylvia, I presume?"*

His eyes bug, and he takes a step back like a vampire confronted by a garlic-basted crucifix. At least he has the decency to look guilty.

For a second. But only one. In the next, the shutters are down and he's adapted this air of casual nonchalance. "Huh?"

"Admit it."

"Don't know what you're talking about. Those are for Sylvia. We have the supplies delivered here."

My mouth drops open, and his brow lifts as he turns back for the living room.

Oh no, he doesn't! "You mean, because she lives here and moonlights as a hunky hockey player?"

"Love it when you call me hunky."

Wait, did I?

Doesn't matter. He shakes his head. "That would be crazy."

Arms crossed, I follow after him as he moves back to the table with the rest of the mail and starts sorting.

"I *knew* there was something funny about our mysterious housekeeper. The way Bowie and Piper always give her so much shit." I gasp. *"They know!"*

That smirk! "You're confused."

"That's how you're playing this?"

"You don't have anything other than the gloves of a hardworking woman." He opens more mail. Tears opens a pouch and spills out some fan mail forwarded from the league.

"Ben. They are men's. Sized extra, *extra* large."

The corner of his mouth quirks. "I mean, that does sound like me. Big. Everywhere. But no. She's a champion weightlifter with extraordinarily strong, capable, and large hands."

He opens the first of the fan mail and— gag —a pair of women's panties spill out.

"Don't touch those," he mutters, lip curled.

I offer the gloves, but he ignores them.

Using two pieces of discarded mail, he sweeps the fan panties of unknown origins into the bin. Washes his hands. Grabs the spray bottle of disinfectant and some paper towels for the table.

"Gross. Do you get stuff like that a lot?"

Shrug.

Wow.

He moves on to the rest of the mail. "Back to Sylvia. In the off-season, she arm wrestles for money at truck stops across the US. She's TikTok famous."

"Ben."

He bites his lip, and it should *not* be sexy. "So maybe the gloves are mine... It— it's a kink!"

"A kink."

Oh my God, the hopeful look in his eyes right now.

"Yeah, it's a dirty, *dirty* sex thing. Blow-your-mind dirty. Dirty AF. Too bad we've just signed a thirty-year mortgage for a house in the friend zone. You'll never see the epic dirtiness."

Arms crossed, I stare at him. Wait for that pull between us to kick in and his eyes to meet mine, because that's how it is with us. And when they do, when I feel that connection lock... *"Ben."*

Those massive shoulders slump on his sigh.

"Okay, look. Bowie and Piper were right." His hand flicks the air. "I can't keep a cleaning service. *For reasons.* But I knew you wouldn't be comfortable here if I didn't clean up my act... like literally. And you should know a lot of those 'reasons'—"

His added finger quotes here suggest those reasons

are vast and varied and possibly in line with the panty delivery of the moment before, but maybe I'm jumping to conclusions.

"—wouldn't be an issue anymore."

"You couldn't get anyone? In all of Chicago?"

"It's about the hockey thing. Have to have a certain kind of service. They actually have to be vetted—"

"How do I always forget you're famous."

"Only a little famous. And I can get someone new now. I will. It's just that you seemed so impressed with how much better Sylvia was doing... so I didn't want to let her go just yet. And—Hell. I'm sorry I lied to you. It was stupid. But that first night when you were going to leave... I really wanted you to want to stay." He sucks a deep breath, lets it go. Shrugs. "There. I admit it. I just wanted you to stay."

I take a beat, letting his confession sit and then my feelings about it settle.

Okay. "So what you're saying is... you're a legit millionaire, professional athlete, who has been cleaning this apartment on his hands and knees... for months. Just so I wouldn't feel uncomfortable here... in this gorgeous space... that you barely let me contribute any rent to... when by all rights, I should be the one cleaning and shopping." At the very least.

He rolls his eyes. "When you say it like that, it sounds—"

"Ben." I press my fingers to his mouth. "You're making it *really* hard not to fall for you."

But I'm not staying. It couldn't last. Right?

Speaking against my hand, he reiterates what we both know. "But that's not what we want."

We.

As in neither of us.

For *reasons*. Different from why he couldn't keep a cleaning service.

I swallow. Nod. "Right."

Ben gives me a wink, brushing my hand to the side. "I'll try harder... to be less hot. Charming. Adorab—" His eyes drop to the half-open package in his right hand. His chin pulls back just as I realize... that's my name on the address label.

No.

"*Champianna Extreme Vibrat—?*"

I shriek, lunging for the box and then racing back to my bedroom... where I slam the door and press my back against it... as I am silently incinerated by the burn of embarrassment.

A text comes in.

Ben: Lock your fucking door

I do.

Ben: If I hear that thing, I'm coming through the wall

I wouldn't use it when he was home. *Couldn't*. Right?

I really, really shouldn't think about it because his threat isn't having the desired effect.

Ben: Make good decisions, Lara

Ben: I'm serious

Ben: What's in the deluxe accessory pack?

Ben: Don't tell me

Ben: Fuck it. Tell me

Ben: Don't...

14

Ben

Lara never texted me back. I've mentioned how smart she is.

And by the time she slipped out of her room, I'd already been out for a run, taken a cold shower, and jerked off. Twice.

Meanwhile, she'd also showered, had her wet hair up in a knot, and was looking a little too contrite for my taste. We ordered dinner. Watched a movie and did not discuss whether her new toy lived up to the waterproof hype. Because, yes. I looked it up.

I know the price. *Damn*, Lara.

I know the specs.

I know about the accessory pack and that if she put it in pair mode, I could control it from my phone.

PS: I installed and uninstalled the app twelve times in the first two hours I knew about it.

But in the end, friendship won out.

Also, I might have screwed something up in my system settings. I can't install anything now.

Whatever. I've been good.

We've been good.

Today, I hit morning skate and knocked a few things off Sylvia's to-do list. Those new gloves? *Chef's kiss.*

I called up a service and got an interview set up for next week. Took a nap. And then got my ass back to Wagner Arena to watch tape, talk to the coaches, and hang out with my team while we prepare to wipe the floor with the Golds tonight.

I did not spend the day thinking about Lara and reminding myself of all the reasons it would be a mistake to try for something more than friendship with this woman. Not the *entire* day, anyway. Just those moments that weren't packed with other things.

Sigh. I'm a work in progress.

Game time rolls around, and I'm jumpy, ready to burn off the conflicting thoughts bouncing around my head and the vast stores of energy threatening to overload my control.

We dress. Clomp down the tunnel to the heavy beat of music and our city losing their minds over their favorite team.

I'm ready to go.

We warm up.

Line up for the puck drop, and it's on.

Head in the game. It's fast from the start.

Head in the game. We're aggressive, but they've got this new kid on the team who's faster than a trending TikTok.

Head in the game. Clash. Whistle.

"Yo, Boomer. How'd you pull that fine piece of ass?"

My head whips around to where Ludkettle is skating past as I give Vassar a hand up from the ice.

Obviously there's nothing incriminating out there, but Lara and I spend enough time together that pictures surfacing was inevitable. I don't love it. Mostly for her. But until now—

"Ignore it," Vassar grunts, back on his blades.

"Right." *Head in the g*—

"Doesn't look like your usual fare. Not the type to exchange favors for cash. Or is she?"

We're lining up again. Vassar doesn't look back when he repeats, *"Ignore it."*

Right. I'm going to. Because my head is in this fucking game.

Only thing, Ludkettle saw me flinch, and the next three periods he runs his mouth. Most of the shit misses its mark completely. But some—

"Girl like that deserves better than some fuck boy one stubbed toe away from washing out of the league..."

"She know how many skanks have taken a ride on that filthy stick of yours..."

"Everybody knows..".

"Least with that rancid nut she won't have to worry 'bout you knocking her up..."

"Maybe I'll take a turn with her..."

—Yeah, some of his chirpy bullshit hit a nerve I didn't know I had.

.

15

Wait a minute, I already read this paragraph. Didn't I?

I get up from the table and stretch out my back and shoulders, both protesting after being hunched over my laptop for the last several hours.

Days? Weeks? It feels like I've been fine-tuning this presentation for the Alexi B account forever.

I should call it quits for the night, trust in the fact that I've done my job right and it's ready to go to my boss.

It was ready before Ben left for his game tonight. Ready when I checked the score and saw they were down by one at the half. Ready when I checked again and saw they won by two, but Ben had spent enough time in the penalty box to merit a mention. And still ready an hour later, when he quietly let himself in, suit jacket folded over his arm, a kind of wired look in his eyes as he pulled me in for a hug and told me he was going to bed.

How long ago was that?

My finger hovers over the send button.

Click it.

It's ready.

It is.

I bite my lip.

Maybe just one more pass.

I'm scrolling up to the top when I hear Ben's deep voice rumbling from his room.

On the phone?

I thought he was tired? And a part of me that really ought to know better is wondering who he's talking to at almost two a.m.

He can talk to anyone he wants. At any hour he wants.

It's none of my business.

I try to refocus on the file in front of me, but now it's the quiet in the apartment that's distracting. Maybe he went back to sleep?

"Are you fucking kidding me, dude!"

The muffled roar emanating from behind his closed door has my head jerking up. And the furious pounding

— *thud, thud, thud* —has me jerking to my feet and on the move before I can even think to stop.

Heart racing, I get to his door just as it flies open. And there he is, so tall and broad he practically fills the door-frame. And the fact that he's shirtless means even if he wasn't monopolizing that space, the chances of me seeing anything other than the hard slabs of layered muscle making up the masterpiece that is Ben's bare chest are zero.

Shirtless Ben sightings have been few and far between since I moved in. Even that one night upstairs at the bar, he didn't take it off. And now I— I can't look away.

Ben pulls back a step, startled to find me there. But then that look of surprise is wiped away by one of pure malice as he carefully pushes past me with a gruff, "Sorry."

"What happened?" I ask, padding after him at increasing speed as he heads down the hall past the office to the laundry room. "Are you okay?"

"Fine," he bites out, a vicious light shining in his eyes as he grabs the broom from where it hangs on the wall. Leaving the dustpan behind, he cuts around me and darts back to his room.

Broom plus shouting... equals ...*bug*?

I whimper once. And for a second, all I can do is lift one foot and then the other like one of those Nature Channel lizards on the scorching dry earth. Because what kind of bug would be big and bad enough for Ben to lose his shit like this?

But whatever momentary paralysis I'm suffering from, I shake off when a new, different thud sounds... this one not quite so dull. In fact it almost sounds—

"Bowie, whatever the fuck you're doing up there..." Ben yells, *"...stop..."*

Thud.

I rush back to his door and skid to a stop, jaw dropping at the sight of a red-faced Ben on his bed, broomstick in hand as he jabs at the ceiling.

"...This fucking minute!"

Thud, thud.

He's lost his mind. "Wha—?"

"And Piper, get your ass down here!" *Thud, thud, thud, thud!*

"Ben." Somehow that gets his attention. His head snaps around, and when our eyes meet, I see the clarity return to his. But his arms are already in motion taking the broom up.

Thud— Crack.

"Uh-oh." He looks up and then immediately ducks as plaster rains down.

Darting forward, I grab his arm, pulling him back, but not before the disheveled spikes of his bedhead are covered in clumps of debris along with his shoulders, arms, and chest. Eyes pinched shut, he lets me guide him down from the bed. The broom hits the floor with a clatter, and another clump of ceiling comes free.

Heart pounding, I reach for his face so I can look. "Did any get in your eyes?"

"Don't think so," he breathes, then louder with more frustration, "*Fuck*, that was so stupid. If I damage my eyes with the season barely started—"

"Hey, you won't." I put as much confidence into my voice as I can, but we both know that another injury this close to getting back on the ice isn't what a career as volatile as his needs. "Just hold on to me and keep them closed."

Blindly, he finds my arm and then my shoulder before dropping his hand to my waist where it stays as he steadies himself.

"Here come with me." I guide him around the bed and into the bathroom. "We're at the sink. Just... um... bend forward... wait... step back... Perfect."

Bracing one hand on the counter and the other at my hip, he hangs his head low while I brush drywall from his hair.

"We've got this. Just a minute more, okay?" There's a lot in here. And that's all I'm thinking about. Not the fact that my fingers are in his hair. That even with all this crap in it, it's still thick and soft. Or that the last time I had my fingers in it, he was inside me.

"Yeah." He heaves a breath that makes his impossibly wide back even wider. "I'm such a tool."

I pause. Then, picking the last of the chunks out, tell him the truth. "I mean, in the last five minutes, you've offered up some solid evidence to support that."

He huffs a low laugh, because that's what he does. First and loudest, he laughs at himself. But I've known him long enough, seen the sides he doesn't always share with everyone, to understand part of that is because it's easier to laugh with someone than to have them laugh at you.

Turning on the faucet, I dampen a hand towel. "Up."

He straightens and faces me. Eyes still closed, hand still at my side, he waits as I wipe away the plaster from his lashes and brows.

"But you're more than a few moments of rash behavior." I run the cloth over his forehead and across his cheekbones. "To me, you're always going to be the guy with the biggest heart, the most creative plan, and the limitless generosity for the people you love. You're the best guy I know."

Above me, Ben's eyes open, meeting mine.

I stop, the towel coming to rest at the hard edge of his jaw.

His brows draw down as he stares at me. "You're the only one who sees me that way."

"Not possible," I whisper, shaking my head because it's so obvious to me, I don't know how anyone could miss it.

The corner of his mouth lifts the barest degree.

God, he's gorgeous. And suddenly I'm aware of just how closely we're standing. Of my hand at his face and his at my waist. Of the slight pressure of his fingers and the rise and fall of his chest. How the second I forget to intentionally hold myself back, the space between us feels like it's collapsing in on itself. Pulling us in. Closer.

Those blue eyes darken.

Closer.

My heart beats heavy. Loud enough I feel like it's echoing through the room.

Clo—

Wait.

I freeze, realizing that rhythmic *bu-bump, bu-bump* isn't my heart at all. If I'm not mistaken, it's the sound of a bed hitting the wall. In the apartment above ours. Where Piper and Bowie live.

"Ooooh, okay. Now I get it."

Ben blinks, a furrow digging between his eyes. His fingers flex again almost like he doesn't want to let go. "You get what?"

Bu-bump, bu-bump, bu-bump.

Recognition.

I make a face, hoping Ben won't fly off the handle again. But he just takes a step back. My hand falls away from his cheek and his from my waist, breaking that closed-circuit connection. Which is probably a good thing.

If I keep saying it, maybe I'll believe it. Or maybe not, because I've been saying it for months, and here we are.

From where we're standing in the bathroom, we angle our heads together to peek out into his bedroom. Another clump of plaster drops with the next *bu-bump*, and Ben's shoulders droop.

"I'll clean it up. Patch it." He circles a hand in the air, looking guilty. "Sorry about this."

He's embarrassed. And exhausted. And probably a little traumatized hearing his best friend pounding his little sister into the mattress. Catching his hand in mine, I give it a light squeeze. "Hey, I was just wrapping something up for work. But it's late. We should both get some sleep."

"Yeah, I'll crash on the couch."

"You can't sleep on the couch." I laugh.

The man is a professional athlete who missed the end of his season because of an injury. No way am I leaving him to the couch *in his own apartment*, even if he is the reason he'd be there.

"Look, you can stay with me tonight. Tomorrow we'll figure out what to do with your ceiling."

He rubs the back of his neck, looking anywhere but at me. "I can't sleep with you, Elliot."

And there it is. The elephant in the room we've discussed, dismissed, and tried to ignore the last two weeks. The attraction we were trying to subdue that night at the bar still burns as hot as ever.

But that attraction is just going to have to take a backseat tonight.

I heave a breath. "You can. You *have*." Not in this iteration of our friendship, but whatever. And just to show him it won't be weird, I add, "But this time, you'll have to stay on your side of the bed. No shenanigans. Okay?"

For a second, I think he might say no. But then he nods and turns to me. "Thanks, Lara."

"It's what friends are for, right?"

16

Ben

Friends are *not* for mauling in the wee hours of the night.

Not when they become some heat-seeking entity that slowly but relentlessly stalks you across the width of the bed.

Not when they burrow into your side and sigh against your chest so you can feel their soft lips brushing your skin.

Not even when they murmur from their sleep of the dead how good you smell.

And especially not when they end up half on top of you, one smooth, toned leg draped over you in a way that has a certain appendage pleading to roll said friend over so your heat-seeking entity can spend some time with hers.

No.

She trusted me in her room, her bed. And yeah, she's pretty much crossed every line there is when it comes to friends sharing a bed, but not consciously. Not because she actually wants something with me.

This is just her body acknowledging an attraction that won't quit but isn't doing us any favors. And no way am I going to abuse that trust by pretending I don't know better.

Yes, she feels insanely good. But I don't want that with her again.

She shifts closer, her thigh riding higher.

Gulp. I don't.

She turns her head, and her hair spills over my side like silk, taking me back to nights from a lifetime ago. Making my fingers itch to touch it and my fists clench. I don't.

I take a slow breath. Then, moving even slower, because I also don't want to wake her up, I try to ease her thigh from where it's currently nuzzled up against my balls. And my restraint— where the fuck are the witnesses because I deserve a medal for the way I handle that creamy expanse of bare skin.

I'm all business.

Just a three-count and then a single press of one hand at a spot near her knee. A gentle nudge that eases her leg clear of my junk, and as much as it pains me, then clear of my leg altogether.

No lingering. No wandering.

Little to no regrets on my part.

All the regrets are from Big Ben who is currently standing vigilant by the window in my shorts, hoping to catch another glimpse of the thigh that got away.

Not me though.

Nope.

Not even a little.

"Mmm, Ben."

My heart fucking stops, and I turn my head toward that sleepy, sexy purr so fast, I end up with a tweaked neck.

"Lara," I answer, my feigned indifference stripped bare in a blink. But all I get back is another soft sigh against my side as she cuddles closer, drawing her knee back to where it was before... And then an inch higher.

Fuck. Me.

I blink down at where she's tucked against me. And then turn my attention to her ceiling and spend the next three hours staring at it.

I THROW my SUV into park and kill the engine behind a brick-worker-style house painted yellow with a yard that's surrounded by a high chain-link fence.

As part of the Chicago Slayers hockey team, every player is contractually required to do a certain number of volunteer and publicity gigs a year. It raises money and brings attention to some pretty awesome causes, and most of the time I feel damn good about having the opportunity to be involved.

But today? I'm so screwed up over the night spent with Lara, I don't know how I'm going to focus on the promo. Which isn't fair to the guys running this place, the PR team... hell, it's not fair to me. I need to get my head straight.

I'm early, so I take a minute to find my calm.

I close my eyes and start practicing my breathing, try to focus on the in and—

Knock, knock.

I turn to where the last guy I expected to see this morning is grinning in through my passenger-side window.

"Static?" I cough as my teammate waits for me to unlock and then slides into the seat, apparently intent on hanging out until our start time. He rubs his hands like it's arctic temps out when midway through October it's not even as cold as our rink.

"Thought Kellog's supposed to be here."

"Something came up and he needed to trade out. I was free." He shrugs, then gives me a once-over. "You look like shit."

I'm not falling for this again, the too-easy-to-talk-to

trap with the prodigal buddy returned. That morning in the gym was a fluke. It was.

Except ten minutes later, he's got his index finger pressed against his chin. "So, if I'm hearing you right, Lara makes you want something more than the transitory bunny action you've been living off for... ehh, as long as I've known you, anyway. But you still know better than to want it from her, yeah?"

Hmm. That seems like a big statement.

When I don't answer, he shrugs. "So why not just consider giving something, or someone other than Lara, a shot. Start small. Like stop picking up dates in parking lots and—"

"That is *not* a regular thing."

He raises a heavy brow because he knows it's not a *never* thing either. At least before the nutastrophe.

I huff. "Take all the women I've hooked up with, and it's a very small percentage. *Very.*"

He rubs a hand over his mouth. Fucker's trying not to laugh. *Dick.*

"Would you feel better if I substituted hotel bar?"

Obviously. "Yes, I would. Thank you."

"Fine. Stop picking up dates at the *hotel bar*, and hell, just be open to the possibility of there being more than one night with the next woman you meet. Maybe you're ready to try commitment on for size."

Am I?

Static taps his phone. "That's all our time for today. I'll be billing you at the usual rate."

I laugh as we get out and head around to the back door of the place. But I've got to wonder if he's right.

It's been months since I had a bunny in my bed. Her bed. A bed. Fine, the front seat of my car. Whatever. It's been months, and only part of that was about my nut. I'd been slowing down anyway. Losing interest in the repetition of something that no matter how varied or creative the sex was... felt hollow. Meaningless.

For a long time, that's all I wanted.

It felt easy and uncomplicated. Safe.

But hey, maybe a little meaning wouldn't be the worst addition to my life. Something with the potential to last.

Static opens the shelter door, swears, and then slams it again... going so far as to lean into it.

"What the fuck, dude?" I push him aside and reach for the handle.

"Don't," he warns, but it's too late. I open the door... to *pandemonium*.

Dogs are barking, people are running, and cages are rattling.

Staff ranging from about fifteen years of age to I'm guessing seventy, all wearing orange T-shirts with the shelter name, are trying to catch... something. It's small. It's fast. It's a blur of black and white, weaving and dodging between reaching hands and shuffling legs as the staff pursues the little beast making a noise like a broken squeak toy.

"Candice, get him!" shouts one of the orange shirts as the blur runs warp-speed circles around his handlers.

Static blows out a low whistle and, shaking his head, takes a wary step back as I step in and to the side.

"Cut him off," gasps an older woman with a long gray braid and a name tag that says "Susan." She bumps the counter and stumbles, so I push in, crossing to catch her elbow.

"You okay?" I ask as she glares at what I'm pretty sure is a dog. He's got a solid case of the crazy eyes, just a little buggy, not quite aiming the same direction. And that tongue... are they supposed to be that long?

"Who the hell thought E.M. was the right dog for this event? Who?!" she snaps, and now everyone is taking a step back.

Damn, don't mess with Susan. "His name is E.M.?"

She growls, and I gulp. "For Eager Much. He doesn't know where he's going, but he sure can't wait to get there. He's... energetic. He's a lot." She *harrumph*s, eyes narrowing on the other staff as they scramble after this whirling dervish. "And whoever thought the least-adoptable dog in the shelter was appropriate to include in a publicity spot needs to get their head out of their ass."

Least adoptable? That's kind of harsh. And "a lot."

That could have gone on the back of my jersey all the way through middle school.

Ben's A Lot.

"Ben's very smart, but he's a lot."

The other staff are breathless, grunting as two of them reach for him at the same time, bumping heads as he darts toward Static who's standing with his back to the wall.

I point. "Dude, *the door.*"

But it's too late. The blur has seen a way out and, sliding sideways as his little paws frantically dig for purchase, he makes a break for it.

Aww, shit.

Not on my watch, buddy.

All I need is some viral TikTok of me letting this dog slip past me when I'm trying to show the fans, management, and the kid bagging my groceries I'm ready to play.

So I channel our goalie, Olsen, and throw myself in front of the door, full extension— *oomph* —sliding across the linoleum so my body blocks the exit. I'm half looking for the phone that's *got* to be catching this shit, because I'm feeling heroic AF.

But unlike the pucks I play with for a living, the blur jumps, using my ribs as a springboard and vaulting to freedom.

A chorus of cries sounds, and then all the orange

shirts are racing to step over me, one of them landing a kick.

Susan, I'm looking at you.

The chase is on outside, this time Static *is* trying to help.

I jackknife up to sit and rub my hands over my face, wondering if this day can get any worse when—

What the—?

I open my eyes and find two paws pressed against my chest. The blur is staring at me from three inches away, one ear straight up, the other flopped down, over-long tongue hanging out the side of his mouth, and tail wagging so hard his whole body moves with it.

I raise a brow and look out at where Susan, Static, and the other orange shirts are checking under cars and behind dumpsters.

I look him in the eyes. One eye. "Really?"

He cocks his head like he's actually listening, and I give him a rub before gathering him into my chest and standing up to let everyone know the blur has been secured. And it's time to get this PR piece done.

17

Lara

After the intensity of submitting my presentation followed by last night's unexpected turn of events, I climbed into bed with Ben, bracing for a sleepless night of vigilantly maintaining a six-inch buffer between us.

Unnecessary, as it turns out. I slept straight through to my alarm at five.

Ben was long gone. The sheets cool on his side. No sign he'd even been there, except for the faint lingering scent of his soap on my spare pillow... which I only sniffed once. Okay, once when I woke up with my nose buried in it. And then once more after I'd showered and dressed for work. But that was just curiosity.

Me wondering how long that fresh mix of spice,

soap, and *Ben* would last, speculating as to whether it might still smell like him when I got home.

A quick search of the apartment revealed he wasn't in the back office or his room or out front.

I hope I didn't keep him awake. I haven't *slept*, slept with anyone in a few years, and for all I know, I've started snoring like a bear, and Ben was forced to retreat to...

A hotel? His sister's spare room? A teammate's place? A hookup's bed?

Wouldn't be a stretch. The man probably has a few hundred women begging to make themselves available at the drop of a hat trick.

Totally fine. Great for him.

I want to mean it, but then I'm chewing my thumbnail wondering what if he decides it's just easier to stay somewhere else tonight too?

None of my business and nothing I have feelings about one way or another.

Gah.

My lies would be a heck of a lot easier to buy if I wasn't currently standing in the open doorway to his room, staring at his stripped bed and swept floor with this betraying knot of dread deep in my belly.

I fill my travel mug and tuck my laptop into my oversized tote. Take a few steps toward the door, debating whether I should text him— when I jolt to a stop.

My presentation.

Oh my God, here I am sniffing pillows— yes, I hit it again —while my project, months in development, hangs in the balance.

It's too soon for anyone to have looked at it. Not before six a.m., but once people start rolling into the office or opening their email on the train, I want to be ready to answer questions, take feedback, and revise as necessary.

Which means, *priorities, girl!*

I race out the door, shoving thoughts of Ben and his mysterious early-morning whereabouts aside.

Two buses and a near miss with a bike messenger later, I coast into GHW to find Fatima, of course, already there. She's striding down the hallway with one of our junior reps, chasing behind with fingers flying over his tablet as she talks.

She sees me and her chic cake-stand heels come to a stop as her smile spreads wide. "Bill, see where you get with this and then catch me after Pilson's meeting."

Bill nods, turning back the way he came.

"Morning, Fatima. Still keeping New York hours?"

She gives me a thick-lashed wink as we fall into step on the way back to her office. "Easier this way."

"Easier when you move to New York in two months. You'll already be used to the new time zone."

She winks, switching gears. "Saw your presentation. Good work."

She's already seen it. Of course she has. And, oh my

God, good work! I'm going to burst. I want to jump for joy, throw up my hand and high-five myself. I want to call Ben and squeal in his ear, but I rein it in, settling for a professional nod instead.

"Thank you, Fatima. This one really clicked for me. It's been a pleasure to work on."

Read: Keep me on the team. Let me take lead, pulllleease!

Lips pursed, she nods.

"It's clean. It's tight. It's got that magical something you bring to every campaign. It makes me *feel*." We stop outside her office door, and she goes to her toes, craning her neck to make the most of her five-foot-one stature to see if anyone else is around. "This is exactly the kind of work I knew you'd deliver. I can't really say more yet, but you're making something I'm working on quite a bit easier."

"Thank you?" I say, thrown off by that last cryptic bit.

Fatima spins on her heel with a flourish and then, looking back over her shoulder, adds, "I've got a client call in five, but if you're free this evening, there's something I'd like to run past you."

~

Lara

I'M STILL PROCESSING what Fatima shared with me over vegetarian spring rolls in her office when I get home.

She thinks my proposal is strong enough to argue that she wants to keep me on her team when she moves up. It's a long shot, but being attached to New York's team while I'm still in Chicago would be a dream

No. I can't get my hopes up.

It's too soon for that kind of offer. It's not going to happen. Not yet.

Ack. I close the door and set my bag by it, slipping out of my heels. There's some noise coming from Ben's room, and I wonder how much progress he made on his ceiling.

A part of me is hoping it's not much and he'll have to sleep with me again tonight.

I'd like to say it's because I slept so well. But if I'm being honest, that isn't the only reason.

There's a part of me that wants to be close to him in a way we aren't as friends.

A part that doesn't care about how much it hurts when it's over.

A part that just wants more, even though I know I shouldn't. A part that wants to ignore that I'm leaving, that I have a plan, that a relationship isn't a part of it... even if Ben actually wanted one. Which he doesn't.

We're friends. Which is fine. It's better. I think.

I sigh, walking toward his bedroom ready to smile and act like I'm thrilled with whatever progress will keep him out of my bed tonight. Halfway there I hear another muted thump, different from those of last night, followed by some sort of wheezing that doesn't sound right.

His door is half open, so I give it a quick knock and push it the rest of the way. There's a sheet of plastic over his bed, smooth plaster above... and about two dozen boxes, bags, and one—

That unholy sound comes again, and when I turn toward the source, Ben's bathroom, a streak of black and white shoots through the room and between my legs.

"What—??!"

But then Ben's blazing past me too. Shirtless, again. Dripping wet. Sexy grin going full tilt. "Hey, Elliot."

My hand goes to my heart, trying to still the hard thud.

"What was that?" I ask his retreating back, following as he jogs down the hall toward the living room where a small beast tears from one end of the living room to the other and back, circles the table and disappears into the kitchen for all of two seconds before reemerging to repeat the whole process again.

"Is that... *a dog*?"

Ben laughs, coming up beside me. "He's getting the lay of the land. Exploring his new digs." Then tipping his head in my direction, he quietly adds, "Didn't have much room to roam at the shelter. Kinda rough start."

As if on cue, the dog starts to shake, like he's a victim in all this rather than the bringer of chaos his grand entrance suggested.

Ben gathers up his quaking beastie and wraps him in a towel, flipping it onto its back within the crook of his huge arm with an impossibly masculine... coo.

And that sound coming from this big brute of a pro hockey player does something to my lower regions that is not okay. At all.

I gulp, watching those blue eyes go soft. Another second of this and I'm in danger of suffering a full-blown ovarian event. Which does not happen to me. Ever. I open my mouth to say something about his rescue, only I'm struck silent by mountains of hard-stacked abdominal muscles and solidly balled shoulders and biceps, all flexing and shifting and—

Ben clears his throat. "Eyes up here, Elliot." Then with a low chuckle, he peers down at his swaddled dog. "Or on *baby*. That's okay too."

Panicked, I glance around at anything other than the pure, unadulterated hotness in front of me.

The dog makes that squeaking wheeze sound again, staring up at Ben in adoration. I think. The eyes, they aren't quite normal.

Carrying the little bundle, Ben walks over to me. "Surprise. He's ours." Then, "*Kidding*. He's mine. But you can pretend he's yours too awhile."

"Umm. Thank you." There's a lot coming at me really quickly here and I haven't quite caught up. "But, where— I mean, when?"

"I was doing some work at the shelter through the

team today. He kind of made a statement up front and...
I guess, they didn't feel like he had much of a shot at
being adopted. I kind of just couldn't leave him.
Someone may have pulled some strings for me to be
able to take him so fast. Dunno. I named him Zamboni.
And sorry I didn't give you a heads-up." He meets my
eyes, and I melt a little more. "Lara, they said he's been
there for *months*. I just couldn't not take him."

God, this man has the most beautiful heart.

"Ben, that's so great." And so sweet, I'm having hard
time swallowing past all the emotion. "I can help with
walks and training and stuff when you're not around if
you like?"

"I've got a walking service set up already, so don't
feel like you need to do anything for him unless you
want to."

I step closer to get a look at Zamboni all nestled in
his arms. Calm. Quiet... And then, instantly, *not*.

"Whoa." Ben whistles down at where he's now
holding an empty towel. "Little dude has some serious
Houdini moves."

We stand there, watching Ben's new dog ricochet
from one end of the apartment to the other, our heads
swinging back and forth like we're at a tennis match,
until I'm laughing so hard I can barely catch my breath.

Ben steps into his room and comes back a minute
later wearing a fitted T-shirt and folding the plastic drop

sheet. He takes it into the kitchen and stuffs it into the bin as Zamboni zips between his feet.

"What do you think of him?" Ben asks, daring a look my way, something in his tone telling me my opinion matters. Maybe for more reasons than just because I live here too.

"He's kind of—" Zamboni circles my leg, and then leaps up to the highest point on the couch, where he stands like Simba from the Lion King.

"Kind of *a lot*?" Ben offers, looking away.

But that's not what I was thinking. I shake my head, heading for the couch. "I was going to say, he's kind of perfect."

I've never had a pet. When I was little, I wanted one desperately. Begged my parents even though they kept telling me no. And then when my dad lost his job and we hit that really rough patch, I finally understood what it meant when they said we couldn't afford one, and I never asked again.

Told myself I didn't want one. That I was too busy. Too transient.

But now? Like this? "Can I buy him some toys?"

Ben's quiet behind me, but Zamboni seems to have run himself out and is sort of swaying on his couch perch, so, I pick him up and give him a cuddle.

Sigh.

And the way he snuggles against me, those big,

really big, not-quite-right eyes giving me a look that melts my heart.

"How in the world did no one want him? How could anyone resist? He's got so much spirit and—"

And Ben's hand closes around my waist, turning me to where he's stepped in close.

"*Oh.*"

"Lara," he says, voice gruff, brows drawn low over eyes that search mine. Eyes that look almost pained and pull at something deep in my chest I've been trying to ignore.

I open my mouth to ask what's wrong, but before I can make a sound, he pulls me in and kisses me.

18

Ben

This wasn't part of the plan. It wasn't something I thought through. Obviously.

This wasn't me making a move for that relationship we already agreed wasn't a good idea. It wasn't even a play for another night of no-strings fun.

It was my emotions, besting me in one vulnerable moment.

It was Lara looking at my new dog and instantly seeing the very best in him when no one else could. And then it was my emotions blowing the hinges off the door to my heart, and from one instant to the next, the need to kiss Lara— feel the press of her mouth beneath mine for one second, two, and then three —becoming more critical than breathing.

And now, it's me wrestling back control from that rogue fucker in my chest.

It's me, reminding myself that I'm in control of my actions. It's me stepping back, removing my hand from her side, and taking a breath before lifting my eyes to meet the stunned confusion in hers.

And Zamboni's. He's still tucked in her arms, looking from one of us to the other and back.

"Sorry." It's lame. Not enough. But somehow I get the sense that Lara understands anyway. "I know I shouldn't do that. It's just—" If she's my friend, I need to be honest with her about this. "Sometimes I want things I'm not supposed to want with you. My rational brain knows it's not part of the deal, that it would probably be a mistake. That we already agreed it wasn't happening..."

She blinks, looking away. Then back with a small nod and a tiny furrow between her brows.

"It won't happen again. Promise." And then because I can't stand the idea of rolling through any more reasons I somehow stopped believing, I retreat. "Look, I really need a shower. You can hang on to Zamboni or put him in his crate in my room if you don't want to. If he's tired, there's a bed and a blanket and... whatever you want."

I make a beeline for my room, grabbing some clean clothes on my way to the bathroom where I strip, muttering to myself about being stupid, needing to have more respect for Lara and her choices, and knocking my shit off if I want to have any chance of hanging on to this girl as my friend.

In the shower, it doesn't get any better. What the fuck was I thinking? Yeah, it felt right in the moment. It felt amazing. It felt like—

Like she hadn't gotten her thoughts straight enough to haul off and slap me yet like she probably should have. Hell, like she probably would have if I hadn't pulled back when I did.

I rub my hands over my face, trying to clear that troubled look she was wearing from my mind. Only it's not going anywhere.

And worse, the more I think about it, the more I realize what an epic asshole I am. I need to go back and talk to her. Make sure she's okay. And if she's not—

"Fuck."

"Ben."

My head snaps up, and I rub the water from my eyes, not quite understanding what I'm seeing on the other side of the glass. "Lara, you okay?"

She shakes her head, and something inside me dies. She's telling me she's moving out. That kiss crossed the line and now I've lost her again. I feel the panic welling fast, am reaching for the glass door as I scramble for what to say to fix this, to convince her I won't fuck up again.

I always fuck up.

But then she's reaching for the door too, wrapping her fingers around the smooth glass and pulling it open as she—

Holy shit. What is happening here?

—steps, fully clothed, into the shower with me.

"Lara," I choke out, too many emotions surging up at once.

She runs her hands over my pecs and up my shoulders to where they fan out over the back of my neck.

"I don't know what I'm doing, Ben."

Her eyes come up and meet mine. Hold. "All I know is that I can't stop... I don't want to."

Lara

RIVULETS OF WATER are running down Ben's face, dripping from the thick spikes of his lashes and splashing on his cheekbones and massive chest. He's beautiful. Powerful. And so incredibly, overwhelmingly irresistible in all the ways that go beyond physical appeal, I don't know how I ever thought I'd be able to try.

Heart pounding so hard I wonder if he can hear it above the spray, I ask, "What if we—"

"*Yes,*" he growls a breath before his mouth crashes

down. He kisses me like a man possessed, breaking only when I pull back, pressing shaky fingers to his jaw.

Head bowed, eyes on my mouth, he shakes his head.

"You don't even know what I was going to ask."

"Doesn't matter." He kisses me again, teasing me with the flick of his tongue. "The answer's yes."

"Yes? No matter what?" It's not true, even if in this moment he believes it is.

"You want me on my knees, Lara? Licking you 'til you scream? You want me to toss you onto the bed and keep you there, coming for a month? You want me to grab that Thai takeout you love from down the street?"

How does he somehow make the takeout sound as dirty as the rest?

He moves to my neck, kissing and sucking at that sensitive skin. Then, mouth at my ear, "The answer is *yes*."

"If I want another night?" It's the easy ask. The one without risk.

Steam swirls around us. He licks the shell of my ear. "Yes."

But if ever there was a man worth taking a risk for, it's this one. So I draw another shaky breath, and ask for what has been building steadily in my heart until there was no way to resist it. No way to deny it. No way to ignore it as I stood in the living room, fingers pressed to my lips, staring at the empty space where Ben had been, asking myself why I'd ever fought it at all. Knowing I couldn't fight it anymore. That I didn't want to.

"And if I want... *more* than one night. What if I just want *you*?"

He presses his brow against mine, holds me against the unyielding planes of his naked body. "Do you?"

"*Yes.*"

The noise he makes in response is half possessive growl, half savage relief as he takes my mouth again. I moan against his lips, opening to the greedy thrust of this tongue.

He kisses me like he can't get enough.

Like he needs this as much as I do. *Not possible.*

His big hands are everywhere, pulling at my soaked clothes, fisting my wet hair. Gathering me close as he kisses me with a thorough intensity that leaves me breathless, aching. Holding me there as he takes my mouth, my heart, my everything. All the things that go beyond the physical, because while that's a part of it... it's the smallest part of what makes this man so irresistible to me.

He molds my breasts, kneading them through my sodden blouse. Playing with my nipples until I whimper, pressing into his touch.

"Tell me you fucking want this, Lara."

"I do. I want you." The words hardly feel like enough. Not when this dam of denial has broken, and everything I've been refusing to acknowledge to him, to myself, is flooding free. "I want you inside me, on top of me, holding me down, and then holding me close. I want my mouth on you and your hands in my hair. I want to rest my head on your shoulder while we watch old seasons of *Schitt's Creek* and *Blindspot*."

"My favorites," he huffs into the scant space between us.

"And then I want to climb on top of you when you won't give me the remote and use unfair methods to get it back. I want to talk and laugh and touch you like you're mine."

I want it all.

Those are the words I want to say, but it doesn't feel fair to either of us. It's too much, too soon. Too many emotions I've never quite been able to put to bed from too many years ago. It's too new and fragile to know if it'll take in a future too uncertain to make plans around... if Ben would even want to.

So instead, I say, "But right now? I want you to take me like maybe you want some of that too."

His eyes snap to mine. *"Maybe?"*

Oh God, I know that look. My body knows that darkening look of intensity, *craves it.*

The hands at my breasts still, moving to the lapels of my ruined shirt and—

Rip.

I gasp, eyes flaring wide as my pussy clenches hard under Ben's break from control.

The look he gives me is pure masculine satisfaction and tips me over the edge.

I need him. Now.

I start wrestling with my blouse, trying to shoulder out of it beneath the spray, but it's like manacles around my wrists. A fact not lost on Ben, who reaches for my arms and brings them up above my head so the shirt is in front of me. I think he's going to free me, but instead he takes the loose fabric and loops it over his head, effectively binding me to him.

Oooh.

It's a loose sort of play captivity, my shirt barely staying up above his shoulders, but the idea of being caught in his hold is very effective.

"*Maybe* I want *some* of that?" he demands, going to work on my trousers, which give way with more ease than my blouse and end up in a literal pool on the shower floor. "Don't think you're grasping the extent of my restraint these past months."

"No?" A shiver of anticipation spears through me as my panties go too.

"It's *staggering*."

Ben's eyes burn over me like a flash flame, his teeth sinking into his bottom lip, pinning down that hint of satisfaction for a single beat.

"I deserve a medal." Then, "From the second you moved in, I've been working overtime to shut down the gut-deep drive to do all of the above and more. So now?"

"Now?"

He dips his hand between my legs, stroking through the slickness, teasing, and spreading it around. "Yeah, I'm ready to hear you come for me again— and not because of that fucking toy."

I can't even deny it. That toy has been tried, tested, and rated five stars.

He pauses, brows knit, and then his smile hooks hard. "Not *yet* because of the toy. But gimme a couple hours first."

"What?" I squeak, but it ends on a whimper when Ben pushes a thick finger inside me.

"There's an app." He strokes deep and then gives me another. "Truth? I'm hardcore intrigued."

So good.

He teases and plays, taking me closer and then easing away. Building the tension.

And God, he's so big between us, the wide head bobbing against my belly. Making me ache to have him filling me. His mouth moves to my ear, and he bites gently at the shell before growling, "How hard do you want me to fuck you, Elle?"

The words do what they were intended to, pushing me over the edge with a cry as Ben strokes me through the spasms and clenching around his fingers.

Then he lifts me against him and steps out of shower, setting me on a folded towel beside the sink. The bathroom is warm and steamy as he ducks from beneath the confines of my blouse, takes one of my wrists and then the other and unbuttons the cuffs.

"Free at last," he murmurs, pressing a kiss to the bare skin of each.

"Perfect." I slide my fingers into his hair and pull him in again. Because I can't get enough. I've never ever been able to have all that I wanted of him.

In high school, I secretly loved him for years, long accepting it wasn't in the cards. That he loved someone else and was probably going to marry her.

Until one day he wasn't.

And suddenly our friendship sprouted wings, soaring to heights I'd only imagined. But even then I knew the limits. Not just that we were heading in different directions, but that only one of us was all in and the other was rebounding with a friend.

Now though?

This is different from that night above the bar.

It's different from those few weeks of wild and new friends-with-benefits fun after high school. I know it is. I can *feel* it.

But by how much?

We're still going in different directions. Still only have so much time before I'm supposed to go to New York.

And suddenly, it's crystal clear. I don't care that it doesn't fit. I don't care that it can't last. Or even if Ben realizes this isn't what he wants after all. I'll take what I can get for as long as I can have it.

Ben grasps me behind the knees. He pulls me forward to the edge of the counter and spreads my legs wide.

And I won't regret a second.

19

Lara

"**S**o fucking wet," he groans, making room for himself between my knees and then dragging his fingers through my pussy and bringing them to his mouth. "So sweet. Be having more of that later," he promises before leaning in for another toe-curling kiss.

Our tongues meet, rolling and pressing together until he pulls away with a pained growl.

The drawer opens beside me, and then he's rolling on a condom as we pant into the charged space between us.

My heel hooks around the back of his thigh.

His hand braces beside mine on the counter. And

then he's there. Notched at my opening, pressing his steely length into where I'm slick and ready for him.

He goes slow again, letting me adjust, catch my breath. Showing more of that award-winning restraint he was talking about until he's worked himself inside me as far as he can go. Until my lips are parted on a silent gasp as he nudges that deepest point of give, making my body pulse and spasm around him.

"So good." So intense.

So achingly, agonizingly amazing having him fill me this way.

"Ben," I whisper, eyes locked with his as he drags heavily back, the deep, wet friction causing my breath to stutter.

"You feel so fucking nice squeezing me like that. Like you're already close," he says, leaning forward as he pushes in again, this time a little faster. Smoother. Oh God, deeper.

Another spasm grips my core, stealing both our breath. "*Again.*"

"Yeah?" He drags back and then slides in, staring down at where our bodies connect. "Like that?"

I nod, urging him with my heel, telling him with my body that I'm good, that I can take him, that I want more. And he gives it to me. Each stroke intensifying until he's shuttling in and out, angling his hips one way and then the other. Making me feel him *everywhere*.

"Never want this to end," he growls, eyes fixed on the spread of my pussy. "But seeing you taking me so fucking deep. Christ, Elle. I can't wait. Need to make you come."

I cry out, nearly there, close enough that my body feels like it's about to turn inside out.

He leans forward that much farther, hitting a new spot inside as he slips his hand between us. Covering my clit with his thumb, he nips at my ear. "Give it to me, Lara."

And the world around us combusts.

Ben

LARA ELLIOT IS in my arms. In my *bed*. Hours after we finished the sexstravaganza— Read: She had plenty of time to sleep off her orgasms and make her way to her own bed if she'd so desired —and she's still tangled up with me.

But I can't sleep. Can't get my heart to stop hammering so hard I'm kind of shocked it hasn't woken her up. Or Zamboni.

Yesterday was a big day for him. And he's still curled up in his deluxe puppy bed with the sherpa burrow cover we got him when we took him out for a walk that turned into a ride to this high-end puppy shop we nearly bought out last night between rounds three and four.

The place was the shit.

Little over the top, but that's kind of where I live.

So maybe I'm gonna have to get a second job to keep my boy in the lifestyle he's become accustomed to in the last eighteen hours.

Worth it.

Lara cuddles closer, and I grin as she breathes my name in her sleep. Hearing it all soft like that, knowing she's thinking of me even now has Big Ben ready for a stretch and some early-morning calisthenics, but pretty sure I wrung her poor body out last night.

PS: The *app* is fucking amazing.

But in addition to owing her some rest, I've got a busy morning with the team.

I gently extract myself from Lara's sleepy hold and slip out of bed. She rolls into the space where I was, feeling around with the cutest fucking frown on her face, and then cracks a sleepy eyelid at me.

"Come back."

"Wish I could." I brush a bit of hair from her face. "Morning skate."

She's back asleep before I stand up. Zamboni is still curled up tight in his bed, so I go straight to the shower, grinning like I just got named to the all-stars game. Because... *Lara Elliot is still in my bed.*

I make my shower quick, pull on some athletic pants and a team shirt, and then lean down to drop a kiss on her brow. She mewls this contented sound that satisfies something deep inside me. Before I can pull away, she loops her finger in my collar and tugs me in for another kiss.

"You going to be home before your game?"

"Yeah. For a few hours."

She bites her lip, smiling. "See you then."

I swallow hard, because that right there was one-hundred-percent girlfriend talk. The kind of heart-achy sweetness I haven't been on the receiving end of for the better part of a decade. And for a minute, all I can do is stare as she drifts back to sleep.

Last night, lying in bed together, she asked me what we were doing. She told me she didn't know what to call it. And I got it.

Yeah, a part of me wanted to slap every label on us I could find. Tattoo her ass with *If found, return to Benjamin Boerboom Junior.*

Yeah, I'm not proud.

But that's the kind of possessive permanent shit that was rolling through my mind. Only I know better. I know Lara's got a lot of priorities, and whatever this is, I don't want her to feel like it's a threat to any one of them.

So I told her, it's new. It's amazing. And maybe we don't complicate it until we've given it a chance to breathe a minute. Maybe we just know it's her and me and no one else, and we have some fun together while we see where it goes. It doesn't need to have a name until she's ready to give it one.

And the smile she gave me in return... well, it was almost as good as seeing her cuddled up in my bed the way she is now.

But then I feel like a fucking creeper still staring at her, and that's not the look I'm going for with this woman.

I scoop Zamboni up in my arms, slip him into his sport chic harness, and hook his matching leash on.

I swing the apartment door open, and he gives up one of his broken squeak toy barks as Bowie steps back, hand up like he was about to knock.

"What the fuck is that?" he coughs, brows up around his hairline. Then he slips his phone from his pocket and snaps a picture. Probably for my sister.

"His name is Zamboni," I offer dryly. "He's my new dog."

The brows go even higher. "When did you get a dog? And how is it possible there aren't forty new pictures on the team text string?"

"I got him yesterday. And..." It's on the tip of my tongue to tell him about Lara. Explain I was a little caught up— in the sheets, in conversation, in breathless laughter chasing little Z around the apartment, and in the mind-blowing fact that in that moment, I was living the *more* life.

The as-yet-unspecified *more* life.

"Lara okay with the new roommate?"

This is it. The opening to tell my best friend that there's something happening with my *other* bestie. I never told him about what happened between us the first time. Didn't tell anyone but my mom. And this time — "She loves him. Thinks he's perfect."

He nods, bends down, and gives Zamboni a little scratch behind his ears. "You bringing him to practice?"

Shit. "Sorry, should have texted. Got to walk him." At the W-word, Zamboni's ears perk up. He's so smart. "Go on, and I'll meet you there."

And maybe by then, I'll be able to use my big-boy words to share that I've got a dog *and* a girl.

Spoiler: I don't.

I try. But I guess that no-naming thing maybe applies to my teammates too.

"DUDE, I meant *a girl*. A date. Not a dog. Not *that* dog." Static groans, clicking the fob to lock his Rover in the player parking area. He's staring at my phone wearing a slightly horrified expression that has my back up, if you want the truth.

"Like take her out for dinner. Join a dating app. The kind without *DTF* in the bios."

Another prime opportunity. But— "Not actually looking to meet someone new right now."

I have someone. I think. And she is all that I want.

"But check me out with the commitment, right? This boy is going to love me forever."

He looks closer. "How old you think Zamboni is?"

I blink. "He's a baby."

"They tell you that at the shelter?"

And then I'm in front of him. "What's with the laugh, asshole. He's young, okay?"

Hands up in placation, Static nods. "Yeah, man. I see it."

"That's right you do."

We start for the door that leads into the building, and Static bumps me with back of his hand, grin going wide. "You know people are going to call him Boner."

"The fuck they are."

"Not me. But they will. Bowie, Boomer, and Boner."

I blink, seriously questioning my decision to re-friend this guy. And he seems to be picking up my intensifying vibe, because he takes another look at my phone and points to the screen. "So cute though. Look at that face."

"That's better."

~

Lara

BEN: How you doing this morning?

It's nine thirty a.m. and I've been up for about an hour. Warm, golden sunlight is streaming in through the windows, and I'm tucked into the corner of the couch in my loungiest weekend wear with Zamboni snuggled against my hip. My laptop is open, my coffee is hot, and I can still feel this man on every single part of me.

I bite my lip.

Me: So good.

Ben: Now I'm thinking about the way you said that last night. 🔥

Me too. And all the reasons he gave me to say it.

Is it getting hot in here?

Ben: How's my boy?

Me: Perfect. We played for a while, had a little walk, and now he's curled up beside me.

Ben: Tell me you're still in my bed. No, show me. Pic pls.

I laugh, imagining his desperate face. Then snap a selfie at an angle that includes both of us and my makeshift workstation.

Ben: Yeah, that's almost as good as the naked version I was imagining. Your laptop was there. Obviously.

This guy.

Ben: Sleep okay?

Better than I have in years.

I don't typically *sleep,* sleep with the guys I go out

with, no matter how far the date actually goes. I tried it a couple times, but it always felt forced. Uncomfortable. Like I was counting down the minutes until it was polite to either leave or gently hint that they leave. Nothing like those few times I fell asleep with Ben all those years ago. And I didn't like that my mind always seemed to make the comparison.

Not so now.

Me: I did. You?

Dots bounce on the screen, then disappear. Return.

Ben: No regrets?

Wouldn't that be nice.

I regret a lot of things. I regret every minute I tried to deny this was coming. I regret fighting what suddenly feels like it was inevitable. Most of all though, I regret not working harder to hold on to my friendship with this man, no matter how hard it was watching him move on.

Me: Not about last night.

My phone rings within seconds.

"Hey," I answer, guilt spilling through my words. "I shouldn't have said it like that. Last night was amazing. Should you be calling? Don't you have team stuff?"

"Break. Was just signing swag before we watch tape, but I'm done." It sounds like he's walking, the echoes in the background drifting in and out. "What do you regret? Because I've got my own list. Wondering how much overlaps."

He makes it so easy to be honest.

"I regret fighting this thing between us. Pretending that first night was enough... that it was all I wanted."

The background noise dies away completely, and I hear Ben sigh.

"I get that. Last night felt so easy. Hard not to ask why we made it so difficult."

"Exactly." God, why couldn't we have just trusted in that connection?

But I already know the answer. It's history. A few weeks nearly a decade ago... with an aftermath that lasted years. At least, for me.

"But what we've got to remember is that we took our time because we cared. Because we didn't want to let some rash decision— even if it turned out to be the right one —risk something we cared about."

I swallow past the knot of emotion in my throat. "Kind of wishing you were here right now."

He huffs a low laugh. "Probably better I'm not. If I had you within touching distance, pretty sure Big Ben would be in the driver's seat. All these mature insights would be stuck in the backseat while I made you come on my tongue a few times."

"Ben!" I cough out with a laugh.

"Come on, we've met, right?" I swear I can *hear* that sexy smile.

We talk a little longer. He wants to make sure I'm still good with the dog-walking service he hired having access to the apartment when we aren't home, and one of the walkers stopping in later this morning to meet me and give Zamboni his first walk.

I am, though I'll ask him tonight if he minds tweaking the schedule so we don't need the service when I'm home. It's nice he didn't presume I'd want to help, but... I do.

A few hours later, the dog walker shows up. He's on time, packing a pocket full of healthy treats and a business card with instructions on how to use the app to track their activity. It's pretty cool.

Me: Walker and Z just left if you want to check the app to make sure it's working.

Ben: Already did.

Ben: Have another app I like playing with though.

Ben: Get your toy.

20

Ben

Lara comes to the game and sits with my mom in my seats. She's been to other games. Sat in Bowie's seats with Piper once and with Misty in Noel's once. But tonight, she's in mine.

My focus is on the ice. The play. The game.

But those handful of times when there's a break and I catch her chatting with my mom, laughing, while her eyes follow me...

Yeah.

A guy could get used to that.

Like he could get used to coming home from the road and finding his gorgeous girl, snuggled up with his dog on the couch, just waiting to welcome him back.

For years, I never wanted it. Didn't miss it.

But now that Lara's in my life again... It's fucking nice.

I send her gourmet pretzel deliveries at work, she sends me pictures of Zamboni standing alert on the couch back, sleeping in a sunbeam, and carrying one of my socks into his bed. Last night she shared a video of him racing from one end of the apartment to the other and back, a tiny squeaky carrot Mel gave him from the corner store in his mouth. I love to see him so happy, but the best part was hearing her laughter in the background.

There's just one thing...

Lara

HERE'S THE THING. No one knows about us.

It doesn't bother me. Not really. I mean, we've never talked about going public.

And I could have said something to Piper or any of the other girls on those nights when we met out at the Five Hole after a game, but when I realized Ben hadn't told anyone, not his teammates, not his friends, not his family... Well, I didn't either.

But tonight, there's a girl.

Okay, we're at the arena and there're always girls. The number of handmade signs propositioning Ben at every game, home *and away* are staggering. And they don't bother me. It doesn't even bother me to know that he's probably been with more than a few of the women flaunting the proposals and invitations.

His past, no matter how fast or varied, is just part of what makes him who he is today.

And today he's mine.

But the chick in skintight jeans wearing what looks like a child-sized jersey with Ben's number barely covering her admittedly spectacular boobs doesn't know that. And she's waiting for him too. That's what she told whoever was on the other end of her phone as she sauntered past, hips swinging hard enough she nearly checked me into the wall. And there's something about her. She's too casual, too confident. Too oblivious to me standing by one of the giant concrete pylons... also waiting for "Boomer" as she speaks into her phone.

"I'm getting wet just thinking about how sweaty he was between us... Those pictures... So hot..."

She giggles and I cringe, trying to convince myself to walk away. Not to listen.

"...They're going to have to put him back on IR after I'm done with him tonight..."

Injured reserve?

My mouth drops open, and I look around to see if

anyone else heard this woman joke so casually about what Ben refers to as the most uncertain, terrifying time of his career. But Piper is chatting with one of the PR guys who's still trying to sell her on a Slayers wedding and—

"...no, I gotta go. Here he comes."

I swing around to where Ben is shouldering past some press, nodding and smiling as they pat the pads he's still wearing. He's beautiful. Hair a wet mess, cheeks still ruddy from those last intense minutes of the game. And even as he thanks the guys complimenting him, his eyes are on me.

Because he's mine.

Whoa. That's some feral attitude surging to the surface of my psyche. But yeah.

Mine.

Ben has nearly closed the distance between us, and my heart is doing that racing, too-emotional thing again. Like it can't wait to get closer.

I can't wait.

I take a step toward him but stop when baby jersey girl bounces in front of me.

"Boomer, oh my God! *That shot!*" She grabs his shirt, going to her toes in five-inch heels. "Sexy as hell and just the way I like it. Remember? *Hard and fast.*"

Ben's hand goes to the bare skin of her midriff, and I stop breathing.

But when I look up, he's still looking at me over her shoulder, brows all screwed up like, who the heck—?

Except then I see it. The lightbulb turns on, and he looks down at her as he uses that hand to *gently move her aside*.

Hello, air.

Been a while.

"Thanks, Red." Her hands are still fisted from when they were in his shirt, so he looks down, gives a little shrug and busts knuckles before turning back to me, grin wide and welcoming as he comes over. He rubs my arm. Squeezes my hand and then holds on a bit longer.

And the way he's looking at me. It's so Ben. So over the top with so much intensity and affection and... *restraint*.

That's when I get it. He's holding himself back.

"Ben?"

He lifts a brow.

"Anyone know we're together?"

The other brow jumps up with the first, and he takes a quick look around. "Nah. They know we're friends. Been careful." He looks down at where he's still playing with my fingertips, winces, and drops them. "Pretty careful."

This time it's my brow lifting. "Bad for your image?"

"You kidding?" He coughs out a laugh. "Bad for *yours*. But for the record, you don't even know how bad I want to kiss you right now."

"That so?" I ask, waiting for his eyes to meet mine, that weird and wonderful connection to lock into place. And when I have it, I reach up and hook a finger into the top of his pads and pull him down into a kiss.

I can feel his spreading smile pressed against mine, holding.

And then we're breathing together, brows touching.

"Elliot, you are one reckless, wild woman."

"Maybe. Or maybe I'm just yours and you're mine… and I kind of want everyone to know it."

There's music coming from the locker room. That old Black Eyed Peas song, "Tonight's Gonna Be a Good Night."

"Noted."

Slowly, Ben starts moving his head to the beat. Whispering, *"I got a feeling…"* as one massive arm bands beneath my ass, taking me off my feet, up and against him as he throws his fist in the air and starts pumping it to the beat as I laugh, clinging to his shoulders while he dances us around.

He's mine. For now, at least. And so I kiss him back and enjoy the ride.

❧

Ben

I LOVE A REALLY CLOSE GAME. Going head-to-head with an opponent for the entire period and then whipping out the winning shot in the final seconds. Nothing beats that shit.

But there's a cost... The press wants to talk.

They don't care that Lara and I had a serious moment out there in the corridor, or that I'm aching to get home to her. Like now. Because there's still more that needs to be said.

Nope. They just want the sound bites. The face time. So before I head back to my girl, I do the rounds, because it's part of my job. I do it well, because making it look like it's my favorite part of the job is also part of the job. And I do it for as long as the PR guys decide I need to... because I love my job... even the parts that aren't actually my favorite.

When I'm done, the guys want me to hit the Five Hole. Celebrate and burn off some of that adrenaline.

Static shoulders into me on the way to the lot. "Bring *your girl.*"

Yeah, yeah. I'll be hearing about this for a while. But not tonight.

"Next time." And then I'm heading home. Texting Lara that I'm on my way. Mentally telling myself to slow the fuck down. A few more minutes isn't going to make or break anything.

It just feels like it might.

There's this urgency in my chest that I don't fucking

know what to do with. I need to talk to her, tell her some things and make sure she understands that not taking our relationship public earlier had zero to do with protecting my image.

Fuck, the more I think about her asking me that, the worse it feels.

I park and take the elevator up to our floor. Let myself in and drop my stuff, leaving it by the front door for the first time since Lara moved in. She's just coming out of the kitchen, Zamboni circling her heels.

Talk about a nice sight.

She smiles up at me and I wrap my arms around her, pinning hers to her sides as I lift her off her feet.

"What's this?" She laughs softly as I carry her back to our room and set her carefully on the bed.

Then dumping my tie, jacket, and shoes, I climb in so we're facing each other, sharing a pillow.

"From the first picture that cropped up of us, I've been freaking out about what it would mean for you. What people would think. The assumptions they'd make about you because of the choices I've made in my past."

"Seriously? Ben, you didn't—"

I shake my head. "I've never cared much what people think of me. There are a million opinions out there. There are pictures. Stories. Some are true, some aren't. A lot are true."

"I know."

"But the idea that someone might judge you for being with me makes me fucking sick to my stomach."

She brushes her fingertips over my jaw. "That's the only reason?"

I hesitate and her brow lifts.

Time to own it.

"At first, no. But now, yes. I swear."

"Tell me about the no part?"

"I think... I didn't want to get ahead of myself. Yeah, the minute you said 'more,' I wanted to go shouting it from the rooftops. I had some deeply possessive feelings. And I wanted like everyone to know we were together. Except I knew it was new. That it was a little more complicated than your run-of-the-mill romance."

"So you wanted to give us a chance to breathe," she says softly, those fingertips drifting down to my chest.

Nice.

"That and... the first time we were together, I think maybe we weren't quite on the same page."

Lara goes still beside me. Then quietly, "You knew?"

"Yeah, I knew. I mean, we said it in the plainest terms. We were just having some fun. I knew it going in... and then... we kissed. And it was—" I swallow, hard. Hold her eyes, because after learning she had doubts, I fucking owe it to her to let her know exactly where she fits in my heart.

"A rebound," she supplies, a stiffness in her tone that has my brows drawing down.

"A *revelation*." And then I huff a laugh, because I must sound like the biggest wuss of all time. "For me. That's what it was. That's what *you* were. And even though it wasn't what we agreed to, I fell so damn hard."

She's staring into my eyes, searching them. And then—

"Hey, Lara, don't cry," I croon, pulling her into my chest and holding her against me. "We were kids. But I just— I guess, back then, I thought maybe there was a chance you were feeling what I was feeling too. And then when it turned out you weren't..." I laugh again. "Okay, it sucked. For real."

"Ben," she whispers, her palm over my heart as she blinks back tears.

"All I'm saying is that I got ahead of myself before. Thought things were one way when they were another. And this time, it feels like there's so much more at stake. I didn't want to rush, and I really didn't want to be wrong. And most of all, I didn't want to lose you again."

There. It needed to be said, so I said it. And hopefully, that's it for the doubts.

She uses the hand at my chest to push me over onto my back and climb on top, so she's lying over my chest. "Ben, you were my friend, and I never, ever wanted to do anything to jeopardize that. So I hid the extent of my feelings for you... for years. I swear, I wasn't just waiting for my opportunity to pounce, but I'd been half in love with you since the day we met."

"No."

She nods. "And then I guess I couldn't quite believe that after all that time... you would actually feel the same way too. I told myself you couldn't... and that if I wanted to stay friends, I'd need to keep hiding it."

"*Lara.*"

"But know this, leaving you and going to school was the hardest thing I ever had to do in my life. And if I'd had any idea that what was happening between us was more than fun, more than a rebound... I don't think I'd ever have been able to go."

Jesus, I'm stunned. On overload to be honest. Because it can't be right. It can't.

Suddenly, all I can think about is all the time we could have had together... and I can barely breathe through the fucking loss of it.

But then something hits me. I take Lara's face in my hands.

"This is killing me, Elle. But I'm going to focus on the only silver lining I can find here. I'm glad we didn't know. Because it would have wrecked me to be the reason you didn't follow your dreams."

She opens her mouth, but the only sound is a quiet crack from her throat.

I nod. I get it.

She nods.

And then, with a heartrending tenderness, she

kisses me. It's soft and sweet, and when she pulls back, I roll her beneath me and do something I haven't done in eight years.

I make love to her.

21

Ben

"And this is what Lara calls his jaunty little sailor suit," I point out from over Axel and Grady's shoulders as they suit up for practice in the locker room a few weeks later.

Axel has the good sense to make all the appropriate noises, but Grady?

That sorry-sounding *"Dude"* just scored him a trip into the boards.

I turn my screen so Grady can't see it and swipe to the next shot for Axel, and Axel alone.

"And this is for riding in style. Lara got it for him. Sometimes he wears himself out halfway through his walk and just lies down on the sidewalk. See how he has his own little apartment area with mesh siding and optional zip-in windshield? Plus, it's got a basket on top so we can pop into the market if we want to grab some ingredients for dinner, maybe some salmon, maybe some kale, maybe—"

"Whoa, nice wheels," Static says coming up beside me to look too. "That collapse to fit in your trunk?"

I'm like ninety percent the guy's sincere in his enthusiasm over how damn cute our dog is and how wicked cool this dog stroller is. But I give him a three-count of side-eye just in case. Then, "It totally does."

"Nice." He sits back, arms crossed, and kind of sizes me up. Not in an about-to-deliver-an-ass-kicking way. He saves that for the ice. "This thing with Lara looks good on you, man. Never seen you like this with a woman before."

No one has. Except Lara herself. And even way back when I was falling over myself for her the first time... it wasn't like *this*.

We were kids who only *thought* we knew everything. Now we're adults who *know* we don't.

"Think it's gonna stick?" he asks, casual as can be. Like he isn't throwing out the biggest question there is, the only one that matters.

"Dunno. Still early days." Which both is and isn't true.

It's only been a few weeks since we updated our relationship status in front of a few dozen cameras and half the WAGs on the team. A few more in private. Add the friend zone, multiply by a decade, and reduce by all the lost years... and yeah.

What I do know? It's good. It's better than good. And already there is a part of me that is keenly aware that I never want to have to go without Lara again. That just like with everything else with me, my feelings for Lara have hopped the express train before ever looking at a map.

I ought to slow down.

I know it.

But I just don't fucking want to.

And there's a part of me that thinks Lara doesn't either.

Ben

OKAY, truth? I'm a limit-pusher.

Yeah, yeah, I fucking love getting Zamboni goofy shit to spoil his sweet little ass. But I also love seeing how far I can push it before Lara throws up a hand telling me, *enough*.

I've yet to hit that limit, but as I adjust the last little details in our ensemble, I've got a solid feeling about today.

Z's little— fine, not so little —tongue lolls out to the

side as he peers up at me with pure puppy adoration that melts my heart.

I snap a selfie, pretty sure I won't have another chance once Lara gets a load of this.

"Come on, buddy." I take his paw in my hand and give it a squeeze. "Let's go show Mommy."

I find her in the kitchen, leaning against the counter beside the fridge. She's thumbing through her phone, her pretty smile turned down and a small stitch pulling between her brows.

"Everything, okay?" I ask from the doorway, my grab for attention forgotten.

She doesn't look up right away, just smooths her features a bit. "Sure. Yes. It's just this Alexi B account. There's sort of a sister account our New York counterparts own, and they want us to come out to talk about incorporating some of what we've been doing from our end on theirs."

New York. It's like Voldemort. The city that shall not be named. At least, for me.

I've been trying not to think about it these last few months, pretending it wasn't looming like a brewing storm on the horizon.

But yeah, that looks like lightning.

I straighten. Tell myself not to be a fucking douche. "Lara, that's pretty cool. I mean, I don't know how it works in your company, but it seems like a good thing to have the people you want to end up working for asking you to come out, right?"

She's still staring at the phone. The little furrow is back, but I can't totally read what I'm seeing in her body language. "Right," she agrees slowly. "Maybe. I don't know. I— I've just got a lot on my plate at work right now, and it's— timing, that's all." She shrugs, giving her head a little shake before setting her phone face down on the counter and looking at me.

Us.

Oh yeah, there it is. *Check out this fit.*

Coughing out a laugh, she pushes off the counter and rounds the island, coming right up to us.

"Are those little *steampunk* goggles?"

Turns out my baby might be a little older than we first thought. "Vet said some sun protection would be good for his cataracts."

"So cool!" She smiles even wider. "And I didn't know they made these little front-pack carriers for dogs." She plays with his back paws where they're dangling from the little paw holes. "I've seen them for babies, but what a great idea."

And then she wants to know if I had to special order it to get straps long enough for my build.

If she should get one that matches.

If it's Burberry.

And what I want to know is how I managed to

convince myself I was living for these past eight years without her.

Because she's perfect. And she's going to New York.

Lara

FATIMA IS up at the ticketing counter at our gate, arranging her upgrade. I'm reading through the existing GHW-NY marketing campaigns for the Alexi Bradford chain of luxury hotels from the last few years, reviewing numbers and targets. Seeing what naturally overlaps with the chic new Alexi B & Co brand already and where more opportunities exist.

Basically, making the most of every minute I have.

We meet with the New York team first thing tomorrow. Then it's lunch at the Alexi Bradford Manhattan Hotel with all the players, followed by more meetings at the corporate offices.

It's a thrill to be on this team. A stroke to my ego and boon for my resume.

And just so freaking cool to have been requested by name and flown across the country to meet in person.

These are exactly the kind of foundational building blocks that support the career I've always wanted. And that's what I'm focusing on. It's all I'm focusing on.

Definitely not what it means that Ben hasn't asked

whether I've thought about the possibility of staying in Chicago. Or how he was so incredibly enthusiastic about what this trip could mean for moving up.

When I talked to my dad on Sunday he went so far as to delightedly chime in that this trip was almost like getting an interview before a job was even opened.

And the support meant the world to me. So why do I keep finding my thoughts circling back to just how very supportive Ben is about the prospect of me leaving, more uncertainty about that unfettered enthusiasm growing every time.

Ben

"HONEY, WHAT A WONDERFUL SURPRISE!" My mom looks like she's just come back from the gym as she climbs out of the car with her yoga mat and glitter cup.

"Hey, Mom." I walk down to the drive to meet her, pulling her in for a big bear hug. My mother is amazing. She's sweet and patient and fun, and she gets me in a way very few other people do. She's been going to bat for me since the first mention of *Ben being "a lot"* in preschool and helped me overcome my challenges for the next dozen years after that. But most importantly, she calls me on my shit, which is maybe... fine, *definitely* why I'm here.

"Was hoping you'd let me take you out for lunch. What do you say?"

She pats my chest and nods for me to follow her up to the house. "I'd say you just showed up without so much as a text, Lara's in New York, and even though you swore up and down it wasn't happening again, you've got the same look in your eyes you had the last time you guys stepped out of the friend zone. Do you really want to talk about whatever's bothering you in a restaurant full of strangers, or is this a conversation better had over a turkey sandwich in the kitchen?"

She gets me.

I nod and follow her up to the house. She tucks her mat into the hall closet before turning into the kitchen.

When she opens the fridge, I nudge her out of the way. "Let me."

Her brows lift. "You really are upset."

"Sit."

I might have come crying to my mother about my problems, but I'm man enough to make her a sandwich while I do it.

She retreats to a stool at the far side of the counter as I pull down plates from the cabinet and start to layer cold cuts on sliced bread.

The drive up from the city should have been time enough to gather my thoughts, but it is what it is, and in true April Boerboom fashion, she doesn't rush me. She just waits, giving me the time I need.

I cut her sandwich in half and drop a pickle spear on the edge of the plate before sliding it across the counter to her.

"I don't know what I'm going to do, Mom." I swallow hard, feeling the weight of it heavy in my gut. "From before Lara walked through my door, I knew she wasn't here to stay. I was sure we didn't have a second chance in our cards. That I didn't want one."

She nods, reaching for my hand and giving it a reassuring squeeze. "It's hard to want to open yourself up to someone when you've been hurt. But sometimes it's worth it."

I heave a breath. "She's worth it. Hard to believe it's possible, but this thing with us is even better than the first time we were together."

"I can see how happy she makes you. Everyone can." She lifts a brow, nodding to the cut-out news clipping held beneath a Slayers fridge magnet.

It's me and Lara after that game. Not the part where I danced her around or even when we kissed, which is what I'd expected the outlets to print. But the moment when our brows touched and we were smiling into each other's eyes. There's so much emotion in that look, it gets me a little choked up every time I see it.

"So what's going on, honey?"

"I can't pretend there isn't more on the line than I meant to put there."

"And you're worried you've set yourself up to get hurt again if she leaves."

"*When* she leaves. Not if. She's going. She's had her sights set on New York from before she set foot in Chicago. And normally that opportunity wouldn't come up for two years, but she's on track to move faster. Eighteen months, maybe as soon as a year. She's *really* good at her job, Mom. She's amazing. You should see the stuff she comes up with, the way her brain works."

"I bet." She smiles. "Even in high school you were always talking about how you liked the way she thought. And *I* liked the way she saw so much potential in things others didn't always recognize."

Yeah, I see what she's getting at there. "Thanks." But then, that anxious pit in my gut yawns wider. "I can't lose her again, but this job, it's not just that she wants it. She *loves* it. She needs the security of a skyrocketing career more than she needs me. Which is rough, because I think I need her more than I need anything."

"Honey, you don't think you could offer her *security*? Have you seen your salary?"

I know I'm an earner. That I make more in one year than a lot of people make in a lifetime. But this thing with Lara goes deeper than that. She doesn't want to depend on someone else for her security. She needs it to be her own.

And besides, "After last year, we both know this career can end in the blink of an eye." I'm thinking *twist*

237

of a nut, but it's my mom so... "But even without an injury, I could get traded, I could lose my edge. I could—"

"You could get struck by lightning or hit by a meteor or attacked by a deranged deer or, or, or."

I'm stuck on the *deranged deer*. "Dark, Mom."

"All I'm saying, honey, is that you can't live your life waiting for the worst to happen or you'll miss out on all the best."

"I know." I do. "It's just that this suddenly feels too much like high school. It didn't when we started out. I mean, I knew we've been headed in two different directions the whole time, but I was fine until this trip. Which is such a dick thing to have to admit, considering I leave nonstop during the season. But now, all I can think is that one year, eighteen months, two years... it's not enough."

"Ben, I know this feels all too familiar. Especially because of how guarded you are when it comes to letting people get close to you."

She doesn't say it, but we're both thinking about my not-so-stellar track record with people I've cared about prioritizing other things over me. Jealousy, another guy, another team, my little sister, my best friend.

Whatever— it's life, and I don't let it get to me the way it used to.

I had a come-to-Jesus moment last year where I was forced to come to terms with the fact that not everything has to be all or nothing... unless you're cheating on me (the ex) or you're the asshole trying to use my little sister to get back at me for daring to be better than him at a fucking game (my childhood buddy, Charlie)... in which case, enjoy your one-way ticket to Nothing-land on the oversold flight in a seat with a broken armrest next to the bathroom. You're never coming back.

But Lara? "It's not just familiar. It's the exact same thing. Only this time, I know it's coming. And I know I've got the choice to get off the ride before it wrecks... but I don't want to."

I want her too much.

My mom leans into my line of sight. "You've got at least a year to figure out how this works with Lara."

"A year hardly seems like enough time to figure out how to make our relationship work when we've both invested our whole lives in careers that intersect but never align... but I want it."

The not having this figured out is making me crazy.

"Ben, think about what school was like for you. Yes, certain things took more time and more work for you to get them. And it was frustrating when you couldn't just get things the way the other kids did. But in the end that effort paid off in so many ways.

"It taught you not to give up. That there is more than one way a thing can get done. And that even though it may not be obvious from the start, if you give yourself some time and space and a little grace... you'll figure it out."

~

Lara

I'M dead on my feet as I haul my spinner bag to the apartment door and laugh at the sounds of Zamboni chuffing from the other side. "Coming, baby."

Letting myself in, I abandon my bag and drop to the floor so little Z can dance around me, sprinting and circling and pressing his little paws to my chest so he can sneak a lick of my face.

I sit there far longer than I normally would, half to give this guy the chance to run himself out a bit and half because I'm too tired to get back up just yet.

The trip was extended by two days, which meant it ended up overlapping with the start of Ben's, and now I won't see him until tomorrow. Not in person anyway.

Even as I'm thinking it, Ben's face lights up my phone.

"Hey, handsome."

"Welcome home, gorgeous. You're looking like it's maybe a good thing I'm not there to give you the kind of welcome-home ravishing you've been giving me after these road trips."

I laugh, waving at Zamboni's puppy cam, recently

installed to ease both our minds about having people we didn't know in the apartment and around our baby. "No. You should definitely be here. Not for the ravishing." Although, now that he's mentioned it— No. Way too tired. "I need you to peel me off the floor and carry me to bed. Maybe bring me Thai takeout."

"That's it. Forget the Colorado game. I'll be there in... four... six hours?" Then he turns to someone offscreen. "Yo, Rux. How long will it take me to get home, flying coach? My girl's too tired to get off the floor and I need to carry her to bed."

"Ben!" I scold, then scooping Zamboni into my arms, I get off the floor and move to the couch.

He's laughing. "Sorry. Wish I was there though. How'd it go yesterday?"

I nod. Think about my answer and settle on, "Good. It went really well."

Normally, he'd already know. We've been in the habit of checking in with texts and calls for months. But while I've been out East, we've barely had a minute to connect.

"We wrapped things up about nine thirty and then the team wanted to take us out. I probably would have offered up a kidney to be able to go back to the hotel and crash, but—"

"But you are part of the team."

"You're familiar."

I love that low chuckle rumbling through the miles. I

look around the apartment, this space that has been ours since that first crazy day.

New York was amazing. The city. The energy. The team.

But I missed this. I love it here. I love this little beastie nestled in my arms. And Ben...

"Hey, Lara. Still there?"

My head jerks up and the phone is my lap. I pick it up. "Sorry!"

"You're fine. But you need to get some rest. Z was out thirty minutes ago, so he's good. Just grab a glass of water, take him back to bed with you, and get some sleep. I won't call after the game tonight... just see you tomorrow, okay?"

I almost tell him then. Say those words that have been sitting in my heart for longer than he could imagine. But as hard as it is, I hold them back. "Can't wait."

I dutifully go to the kitchen to get the prescribed water but stop in the doorway when I see the biggest, most beautiful arrangement of long-stem roses centered on the island with a little stuffed bear wearing a Slayers jersey with Ben's number on it.

My phone pings again, and I grin, expecting a text from the sweetest man alive.

But it's a call, and it isn't from Ben. It's from the New York office.

～

Ben

Man, travel has never been tough for me before. It's been part of the job, sure, but always kind of an adventure too. What am I going to see, where am I going to eat, who am I going to meet?

And yeah, that stuff is still cool. I like getting to hang out with my buddies from other teams here and there. It's fun to hit a club or get a taste of something that isn't available in Chicago. But lately, I can't help but feel like something is missing.

Like I wish I could share it with Lara.

I want to see how she likes the artisanal ice cream place and watch her eyes close as she listens to the music at the club. I want her to meet my buddies from around the league, and when the night is over, I want to take her back to my room and hold her in my arms until morning.

Okay, I want to fuck her senseless first. Make her come against every horizontal, vertical, and humanly accessible angle in the room. And then I want to hold her in my arms through the rest of the night. And after we walk Zamboni through the city— because, yeah, I'm bringing my boy —I want to do it all again.

Spoiler alert: It's not happening.

That's not how it works in the NHL. We don't bring dates on the road. It's not new. What is new... is that for the first time in my career, I really, really wish we could.

But now I'm back in Chicago, and instead of Bowie driving me home so I can relax, unpack, and snuggle my dog, I've got him dropping me at Lara's building so I can take her to lunch, hear about New York, and ask her about her vacation time and which of the cities I spend my season hopping around to she'd like to visit first. It'll be her and me and Zamboni on an epic road trip for three.

Shit, maybe she'd actually like a *road* road trip. We could rent an RV. Something deluxe. Tour the highways and—

"Welcome to Giles, Hall, and Wren. Can I help you?" a guy who looks like he could be my dad says from behind the front desk. I've been here before to pick Lara up, but usually it's after hours when reception is gone for the day.

"Ben Boerboom, here for Lara Elliot. I'm a little early but we've got a—" I'm about to say date but catch myself in time. This is her place of business. "Lunch."

"Ms. Elliot is in a meeting, but if you'll have a seat, I'd be happy to get you a coffee while you—"

"No, no." A petite woman with a no-nonsense air about her breezes in, waving off the reception guy's words before he's finished them. She gives me a wide smile and holds out her hand. "Boomer? I'm Fatima."

Feeling a little starstruck at meeting Lara's mentor, idol, and favorite person to talk about, I kind of want to pull her in for a hug and ask her to sign my shirt or something. Got a couple Sharpies in my suit pants, after all. But since she's got her hand out, I shake instead.

"Nice to meet you, Fatima. Lara says great things about working with you."

She hums, starting down the hall and motioning for me to follow. "Likewise. So Boomer, this wouldn't happen to be a *celebratory* lunch now, would it?"

Huh? Something tells me she's not referring to the Slayers win last night. "Went that good in New York, huh?"

Maybe my girl's going to score herself a corner office in these fancy digs.

She laughs, giving me a knowing wink. "Lara's promotion, obviously! Don't worry, it's fine that she told you. No secret. She's so talented. Creative. Dedicated. I adore her and adore that she's been given this honor. She's earned it."

And now I'm grinning too, looking up and down the hall for her, like she'll suddenly be there, ready to jump into my arms. Except, *meeting*. Right.

"That's fantastic!" She must have wanted to surprise me with the news at lunch. "She's got to be thrilled. I know what this job means to her."

Fatima stops beside a small conference room with a couple comfortable chairs and a low coffee table, and ushers me inside. "It shows. No one's ever been promoted from Denver to New York so quickly. But that's our Lara. Shooting for the top, nothing getting in her way."

And then I get it. Not a corner office. At least not in this building.

New York.

"Amazing." I nod, a little stiffly, maybe, but I keep my smile up like the PR machine I've been groomed to be, despite the fact that my head is about to explode, and there is something truly unpleasant happening in my chest.

Fatima tells me to make myself comfortable. The meeting should be wrapping up.

Blah, blah, blah.

I nod. Smile again. And when the door closes, I drop into an overstuffed chair and push the heels of my hands into my eyes.

Lara's going to New York. She's leaving.

Thank God I didn't stop at home to bring Zamboni along. Don't want him to see me like this.

Hell, I don't want Lara to see me like this either. She gets a promotion, and I'm sitting here on the brink of hyperventilating.

Fuck. I thought I'd have more time. We'd have more time. But since that's not how this is going down, I need to get my shit together and get on board the celebration bus.

I know what Lara's career means to her. And because

she means *everything* to me... By extension, her career does too.

It's basic relationship math.

I don't know how long later, the door to the conference room opens and Lara steps in, quietly taking my hand and giving me a smile that isn't nearly as bright as it should be. She's nervous. About how I'll take it. What it'll mean.

I want to pull her into my arms and swing her around to reassure her, but since she's gone for a limited hand-holding thing here at the office, I hold back.

"I'm sorry you had to wait."

"Nah, I'm fine waiting." It's true.

I'd wait years for this woman if it meant that in the end, I got to keep her.

"Well, Fatima told me to take the afternoon off. So..." She trails off, her focus getting lost in some middlespace where I can't quite read what's going on. But then she's back with a little shake of her head.

"Elle?"

"Sorry. I"— she searches my eyes and then looks away, and that first stitch of unease threads through my gut —"Just a lot going on this morning. A lot on my mind. I'm fine. Let's swing past my cube to grab my stuff, and then I'm yours for the rest of the day."

I squeeze her hand, drawing her closer, wanting her eyes back on mine. Wanting her bright smile. Wanting her to know we're okay. "Perfect. We can spend it cele-brating."

Her brows furrow. Then she stands a little straighter and I can almost see her arranging her face into a mask of enthusiasm that sets off every alarm I have. "Oh, yes. I — I know I said congrats on that game last night, but I didn't realize what a big deal it was. Everyone was talking about how you played and that shutout, right?"

What the hell?

22

Lara

Please let me be making the right decision.

I spent the night and then all morning wrestling over what to do. Circling around one way and then circling back the other. And while all I wanted to do was talk to Ben about this, I didn't feel like I could. Not while he was out of town.

Same with my dad and Fatima. I already know what their opinions will be, and I know that neither one of them will be able to understand the reason this decision isn't as cut-and-dry as they would like it to be.

I love Ben. I love him like I've never loved anyone or anything in my life. And I can't lose him again, even if it means giving up a professional goal that meant something to me too.

Only now that I've made the choice, now that I know what I'm going to tell New York when we have our call tomorrow... there's something off about the way Ben's looking at me. And after making what feels like a monumental decision, all I want is to see the same barely banked fire and depth of emotion in his eyes. But it's not there.

When we get outside, instead of sweeping me into a hug or planting a serious kiss on me, he seems... stiff. Hands going into his pockets instead of my hair. Watching me with this look I can't quite read but doesn't feel right.

"Everything okay?" I ask.

"Yeah, great. You?"

"Great."

We get lunch at this place a couple blocks down from GHW and... more weirdness. My stomach is in knots, and this sense of dread is pooling within me. Because something isn't right.

We talk, but it feels off and wrong and like something I can't understand because everything was amazing before my trip.

This week we haven't been in touch as much as we normally are when he's on the road. We've both been distracted by the demands of our own careers and... I thought we were fine. But now that I'm back, I don't understand how the space between us that always seems to be evaporating at an exponential rate suddenly feels cold and unyielding. I don't get why we're asking the kind of polite, superficial questions we retired from our conversations months ago. Why every time I try to breach that space, he takes a step back and asks me another weirdly polite question.

"So the flight was good."

"Yep."

"Terrific."

God, am I making a mistake? Is Ben even going to want this?

We get home and the weirdness is contagious. There's window-staring. Him. Me.

Even Zamboni seems confused, his sweet eyes shifting from one of us and back to the other. Tongue lolling like a question mark. And when he pulls one of Ben's socks out of his burrow bed and brings it into the living room, we both suggest a walk. It should be a return to the usual *easy* that we've been waiting for, an opportunity for me to bring up New York.

But no.

Tension is radiating off us in waves as we let Zamboni walk as many city blocks as he likes and then bundle him into his little chariot when he tires.

And by this point my mind has started to spin with the kind of nonsense I know better than to believe...

Maybe he feels like I was ignoring him.

Maybe the days apart gave him some perspective he

couldn't get when we were seeing so much of each other.

Maybe he doesn't feel the same way about me he did when I left.

But I can't believe that's true.

I know it's not.

On the walk back, I keep watching how Ben shoulders are ratcheted so tight they look like they are going to snap. I'm officially freaking out.

Up ahead is Mel's Corner Market. Ben cuts me a look, one brow pushed high in silent question...

Want to stop?

I reply with a listless half nod, half shrug.

Zamboni stands inside his three-season porch on wheels, wiggling his body from head to tail and making the decision for us. He *loves* to shop.

Mel's behind the counter ringing up some guy when we go in. Her eyes light up, and she shoves the change across the counter before shooing her patron out with a scowl.

Climbing down from her stool to come around the corner, she ignores Ben and me completely, as usual.

Then it's all, "*Baby!*" and "*Did you miss me?*" and "*Have I got a special treat for you,*" as she takes the stroller from me and begins pushing our dog through the aisles, telling him about all the products, picking items off the shelves at random and holding them close to the mesh so he can smell each one.

Ben's shoulder brushes mine, and we turn to each other with a private smile, and in this one unguarded moment, the ease and connection that is so much a part of our relationship surges back in. He searches my eyes, an almost wounded look in his before he shakes his head and stalks toward the cold beverages.

That's it.

I can't take it another second. The sweetness layered beneath this bullshit is more than I can stand.

Stomping after him, I take the Eye-C-T he's pulling from the cooler and return it.

"I don't even want the tea."

His head swings around and this time, there's no imagining the devastation etched in the lines of his face. "You don't *want* the fake tea?"

My temper erupts.

"What the hell is wrong with you!"

~

Ben

I BLINK. Blink again. Start to sputter as the half dozen responses that have been locked in my chest all day start climbing over each other, fighting for freedom all at once. Then fucking get a hold of myself, and demand, "Are you breaking up with me?"

Her chin snaps back. "What?"

"You told me you stopped drinking the fake tea when you didn't want to be reminded of me... and now... you don't want the fake tea! So is this it? Because if it is, it's going to be really fucking awkward when I'm in New York this summer and we're broken up!"

She coughs, eyes wide. "When *you're* in New York? Ben, what are you talking about?"

"I bought an apartment in New York!" Talk about an epic fucking miscalculation in that fifteen-minute window following Fatima's celebratory announcement.

Except I can't believe it was a mistake. Can't accept that Lara doesn't—

"Ben!" she gasps, clutching the cooler handle like it's the only thing holding her up.

And now I'm jealous of a convenience store cooler handle, because I want to be the one she leans on. I want to be the one she talks to. I want to be Lara's *one*.

New. Low. Achieved.

"Fatima told me about your promotion, and ..." Fuck it. "I didn't want you to worry about having to find a roommate or temporary living arrangements falling through."

"Y—you bought me an apartment? In *New York*? So —" Her slender, pretty neck works up and down. "—I wouldn't worry?"

She's emotional. And it's making me emotional, stirring up all the shit in my chest that feels like it only exists when she's in my life.

"I know how much having a homebase means to you." Jesus. I can feel the tips of my ears starting to burn. "So I got you one... I got us one... You one."

Her breath is coming harder, faster. Because who does that? What's wrong with me? God, she's got to be thinking I'm *a lot*.

I start to scramble, "But it's like, a good investment, so if you don't like it or want it—"

"Ben?"

"Yeah?"

She slowly shakes her head, eyes holding with mine in a way that makes me hold my breath. "I love you."

My breath gusts out. Relief. I nod. "I love you too, Elliot. I've loved you since we were eighteen years old."

There's a part of me that still can't understand how she didn't know it. Couldn't feel it.

She smiles. "I've loved you since we were fifteen."

Jesus. My heart feels like it's about to pound right out of my chest.

"If I'd known. *Elle*, if I'd known, I would have—" I can't even tell her all the ways our lives would have been different, the lengths I would have gone to hold on to her, to protect what we could have been. Fuck. The loss of those years we could have had together is too brutal to acknowledge.

"Yeah, me too," she admits quietly, hitting me with a bittersweet pang.

And just like that, we're on the same page again. It's

her and me... and Zamboni offering up an enthusiastic wheezy bark at something a couple aisles over.

This is all I want. Everything I need.

I heave a breath, leaning my shoulder against the door. "Why didn't you tell me about the promotion?"

It's been killing me.

"I was going to tell you. I was just trying to figure out how to do it without making you feel like I was forcing something in our relationship, or pressuring you. I didn't want you to feel obligated."

I don't get it. "Pressure me to what, do the long-distance thing? Lara, I don't think you—"

"Because I'm not taking it. There's a call set up tomorrow, and I'm going to tell them no."

At first, the words don't compute. I can't understand what she's saying. And then my heart is pounding with a new urgency, because this is *not* okay.

"Why the fuck not? This is what you've been working toward since high school. You are amazing at your job. This promotion is everything you wanted."

She shakes her head, and suddenly I know what she's saying before the words pass her lips.

"It's not everything. Not anymore."

It rocks me to my foundation. Knowing she picked me over her dreams, it's fucking humbling.

And I can't let her do it. "I don't want to be the reason you give up what you love." I won't.

She's shaking her head. "You wouldn't."

"Okay, then I don't want to be the reason you cut off your dream at the knees."

I've already lived my dream, met my goals. I would never want Lara to miss out on that.

"Ben, I love *you*. And I love that you care so much about me and my goals that you'd want me to pursue them, even if it meant letting me go. But—"

Whoa, whoa, whoa.

"No. I'm talking about supporting a long-distance thing for *a while.* Year, maybe two. Critical clarification there. Let you go *physically*, for a *limited duration*, with lots of conjugal visits that involve the replastering of walls after."

One pretty brow lifts. "Conjugal?"

"Yeah, as in for married people. Because I want my ring on your finger, Lara. I want you to have my name or like a hyphen. Fuck it, I'll take your name, but only because you're so amazing."

"Ben, you're getting ahead of yourself, don't you think?"

"You don't want to marry me?"

"Of course I do! But someday, when you've had a chance to think about it. When you know it's what you want."

I step carefully here. This is too important to stumble over my words and accidentally say something I don't mean. "That's the thing, Lara. Elliot, Elle. I've known I wanted to marry you since prom. *I told my mom.*"

That open-mouthed gasp is the perfect opportunity to steal a kiss, a quick and dirty one, since little Z is still an aisle away.

"Lara, understand me. I want to be with you. I want you to be mine, and me to be yours... *in here.*" I press my hand to her heart. "No matter where we are physically. So I'm in Chicago for the season and you're in New York. We can make it work. There are eighty-two games in the season, I'm traveling for forty-one. Fifteen percent are in New York. We can make this work."

"Maybe they'd let me work from Chicago part of the time."

"And I'll live in New York in the off-season." A lot of guys don't play where they live. And it's not forever. "We'll share a Google calendar. It'll be hot."

She's nodding. Which is fucking good.

"I know what it means to live without you. *Really* without you. It wasn't living. It was existing. Passing time until you brought the meaning back. And I *never* want to live that way again. I want to text and talk and laugh and love. I want to find every minute we can to share space, but even when we can't... I want us to be *together*. Does that make sense?"

She's nodding faster, her smile gone watery. Her lashes dark. Beautiful.

My instinct starts tapping its stick.

Yeah, I know, buddy.

I reach into the cooler and grab a can of Eye-C-T with one hand and then wrap my arm around my girl. Lifting her so she presses her face into my shoulder and her toes dangle as I walk toward the front of the store, I keep talking.

"I know hockey isn't the most secure career choice, and stability is important to you. There's risks even if you don't get hurt on the ice. Last season was a scare that had me thinking about backup plans, about what was next... even before you. But so you know, I'm going to get my degree in education, and when playing this game doesn't feel like the right choice anymore, I'll get a job teaching and coaching at the high school level."

She lifts her head, and I'm pretty sure those are tears on my shirt. "You want to teach?"

"You know I fucking love math."

That smile.

"You really do."

"And I figure we'll be fine on a teacher's salary plus yours. Plus, the rainy-day fund has about ten in it." It's more. A lot more, but I don't want to sound braggy when I'm trying to lock Lara down.

"Ten?"

"Million."

She blinks. But hell, I've been cleaning my own bathrooms... where does she think the money's going?

"And there's also the private island fund. And

Zamboni's fashion fund, but the trust I set up for his care can't be touched."

"A trust," she repeats, dryly.

"You know, in case something happens to both of us. I made Static the executor. But I'm offtrack. All I was saying, is that if you put your faith in me, I swear I'll support your ambitions, priorities, and dreams no matter what. We'll find a way. Together. I want you to have everything."

"Ben—" She squirms a little, and I set her down at the front of the store and place the Eye-C-T on the counter by the register. "What if... all I need is you? What if you're what makes me feel secure, like, no matter what happens... so long as I'm with you, I'll be safe."

"Lara, you've got me." She's had me since we were eighteen years old. She took my heart. And no one ever had a chance at it again. "I'm about to do something rash, but I swear I've never felt more sure about anything in my life."

She lifts a brow... and I sink down on one knee. "Marry me, Lara. You're the girl who taught me what real love was, the friend who reminded me it was worth fighting for, and the woman I want to spend the rest of my life with."

And then because I mean it and I don't want there to be any loopholes after she says yes, because she's one hundred percent going to. Okay, ninety-eight. I swipe a

Ring Pop candy ring from the bin on the counter, rip off the wrapper, and hold it up to her.

She looks at the sucker and back to me, blinking fast, she sinks to her knees and throws her arms around me. "It's perfect. I love it."

"Yeah?"

She bites her lip. "Yeah."

"You're going to marry me?" This is nothing to mess around with. I need a solid yes.

"Oh, yeah." Her hand bunches in my shirt. "I'm going to marry you. Put a ring on it, please."

I laugh, pulling her onto my lap. And then slipping the plastic band over her pinky, I grin like I've never grinned before. "I love you."

She kisses me. "I love you too."

EPILOGUE

Off-Season

Ben
New York

This apartment is the shit. Tall ceilings, great light, and a kick-ass kitchen that's only been covered in a fine layer of flour once since we moved in, and then only because Lara distracted me while I was trying to make my mom's scratch pizza recipe for her. The takeout we got after was great, but the snack I made of my girl *before* it arrived was Michelin-star worthy.

Yeah, I love Chicago too, the fans, and my team, but after we got eliminated in playoffs, Lara and I grabbed our bug-out bag— Z's Louis V travel crate —and flew home to New York. Zamboni loves it here and tore through the halls and around the furniture, wearing himself out, while I proved once again that my impulsive apartment purchase had great bones.

Totally stood up to the test of me trying to fuck my beautiful bride right through them.

Yep. We're married.

Upgraded Lara's ring and everything, though we totally saved that first one. It's preserved in a solid resin block we keep on the mantel in the bedroom.

Lara took the promotion and is killing it in her new position. She was able to negotiate a deal where she works remotely from Chicago when the Slayers are at home and works out of the New York office when we're away and through the off season. So as far as the long-distance thing goes, we're total #Goalz.

Zamboni lifts his head from where he's curled up against my side on the couch, and a second later the front door opens and Lara walks in.

"How was work, Mrs. Boerboom?" I ask, setting my laptop aside.

"Busy, good. Whatever."

Whatever. I lift a brow, and she sets down her bag and phone with a laugh. "Ben, don't tease me!"

She's got her hair twisted up with a few strands falling around her pretty neck, and a pair of wide-legged pants in pale blue that swing wide when she walks. Mesmerizing.

"About what?" I'm playing dumb, but she knows better.

Her lips part on a smile as she slides onto my lap, wrapping one arm around my neck and giving Z a little scratch with her free hand. "The math test. I know you got your results back."

"Oh that." I grin, burrowing into the spot between her shoulder and ear for a little nibble. She's talking about the discrete mathematics and number theory course I'm taking for my teaching degree.

"*Ben!*"

Love it when she says my name. And as much as I like keeping her on the hook, I'm too pumped not to spill. "Aced it."

She lets out a delighted little whoop and gives me a firm kiss. And when my arms wrap tighter around her, a softer one. Slower. Deeper.

We tangle into each other, pulling closer. Fingers sinking into hair. Hearts aligned and beating in time as her hips start a sinuous tease that has me gripping the armrest hard enough it creaks.

"Ben," she murmurs, a hint of laughter in her tone.

"Sorry, sorry." New furniture. "I'll be careful."

Her head lifts, and I'm confronted by one arched brow and her sternest look. "You better not."

Jesus, this woman is perfect. "Okay, I won't." And because her hips haven't stopped moving and this rhythm is really working for me, it's not entirely show when I grip again, getting a louder creak.

Satisfaction lighting her eyes, she bites her lip in that way that promises all naughty good things to come. "*Elle*, tell me what you want."

She rocks again, playing with the buttons of her blouse before slipping the top one free.

I lean in to lick that freshly exposed bit of skin. Follow the lacy edge of her bra as far as the remaining buttons will allow. Her breath is coming in soft little pants through my hair and—

"What happened with the couch?"

Working the remaining buttons because I'm on strict orders not to rip off more than one a month and I hit my quota last week, I assure her, "It's fine. Sturdy. Just a little creak."

"No," she pants against my temple. "Not this couch. *The couch*."

I stop. Look up.

Yeah, she's talking about the couch that used to reside in Axel Erikkson's place before he found out he was having a kid... in two hours... and made that deal with Nora to be his nanny.

"Nothing like whatever you've heard." The rumors around that couch are wildly exaggerated. Mostly.

But if I think that's going to reassure my girl, I'm wrong. "What's that face?"

She shrugs. "I'm just a little disappointed, that's all."

I cough. "What?"

Another lip-nibble. Another swivel that has me seeing stars. "Kind of exciting to have landed the man capable of destroying a couch in a single night. I had ideas, not gonna lie."

Blink. Don't ask. Don't— "What kind of ideas?"

She pulls me closer and whispers in my ear. My jaw drops and I pull back with about a nanosecond to spare before I lose total control.

And there she is, my best friend, my wife, the love of my life... giving me this faux innocent look that works almost as well as the words she's been whispering. "That all?" I croak, fists balling in the sides of her fancy trousers.

She pauses. "And then, I want you to..."

She whispers the rest, Big Ben straining to hear the delicious filth coming out of her sweet mouth. When she pulls back to look at me, eyes a mix delight, curiosity, and dirty intent, I crack, flipping her beneath me on the couch that is about to become the stuff of legend.

This fucker from the Ralph Lauren collection is going to be in pieces by the time I'm done making Lara come.

I'm trying to be careful with her shirt, because rules, but then she growls and rips mine. Whoa.

My heart is slamming so hard I swear they can hear it hammering across the street.

Only then I realize the hammering isn't coming from my chest. It's the front door. And it's loud.

Lara and I freeze, eyes locked in silent communion... *Can we ignore it?*

But Zamboni, who's made his way over to his matching doggie daybed, is now losing his ever-loving mind, racing to the door and springing around doing that broken squeak toy bark.

Lara pats my chest, and I climb off her, adjusting my junk as I walk to the front of the apartment. Whoever this is, they're off the fucking island for good. Dead to me.

I swing open the door, ready to say just that, when Static— who I'd have sworn was in Chicago this morning —barges past me.

And my man looks *rough*.

***

Thank you for reading DIRTY FLIRT! Want more of Ben & Lara? Find their bonus scene at miralynkelly.com/bonus-scenes

And Static is up next! Preorder DIRTY FIGHTER at miralynkelly.com/dirty-fighter

ALSO BY MIRA LYN KELLY

SLAYERS HOCKEY

DIRTY SECRET (Vaughn & Natalie)

DIRTY HOOKUP (Quinn & George)

DIRTY REBOUND (Rux & Cammy)

DIRTY TALKER (Wade & Harlow)

DIRTY DEAL (Axel & Nora)

DIRTY CHRISTMAS (Noel & Misty)

DIRTY GROOM (Diesel & Stormy)

DIRTY D-MAN (Bowie & Piper)

DIRTY DARE (Gulls & Cam)

DIRTY FLIRT (Boomer & Lara)

DIRTY FIGHTER (Static's Story)

BACK TO YOU

HARD CRUSH (Hank & Abby)

DIRTY PLAYER (Greg & Julia)

DIRTY BAD BOY (Jack & Laurel)

THE DARE TO LOVE NOVELS

TRUTH OR DARE (Tyler & Maggie)

ACKNOWLEDGMENTS

Fun fact: There's more to creating a book than just writing the words. A lot more!

The magic that goes into each book that finds its way onto your eReader or shelf extends from that first willing ear to beyond the last set of eyes checking for typos. And I am beyond grateful for every single one of the people continually proving that writing is a team sport.

So huge thanks to Lexi Ryan, Jennifer Haymore, Zoe York, Skye Warren, Najla Qamber Designs, J. Ashley Photography, Wordsmith Publicity, Tara Carberry and the team at Dreamscape Media, and Nicole Resciniti. To all the girls from Write All The Words, the Book Bunnies, my Promo team and Eagle Eyes, and the reviewers and bloggers who help me spread the word about my books. To my family who puts up with my crazy hours and pig pen office and my friends who are the best break from deadline crazy.

And especially to you! Thank you for reading.

((HUGS)) Mira

ABOUT THE AUTHOR

Hard core romantic, stress baker, and housekeeper non-extraordinaire, Mira Lyn Kelly is the USA TODAY best-selling author of more than two dozen sizzly love stories with over a million readers worldwide. Growing up in the Chicago area, she earned her degree in Fine Arts from Loyola University and met the love of her life while studying abroad in Rome, Italy... only to discover he'd been living right around the corner from her back home. Having spent her twenties working and playing in the Windy City, she's now settled with her family of eight (including two ridiculous dogs) in beautiful Minnesota. www.miralynkelly.com

Looking to stay in touch and keep up with my new releases, sales and giveaways?? Join my newsletter at miralynkelly.com/newsletter and my Facebook reader group at MiraLynKellybookbunnies. We'd love to have you!!

Made in the USA
Monee, IL
05 July 2024

61227648R00163